The First Person

The First Person

Péron Long

URBAN
Renaissance

www.urbanbooks.net

Urban Books, LLC
78 East Industry Court
Deer Park, NY 11729

The First Person ©copyright 2010 Péron Long

ISBN 13: 978-1-60162-205-1
ISBN 10: 1-60162-205-8

First Printing May 2010
Printed in the United States of America

10 9 8 7 6 5 4 3 2 1

This is a work of fiction. Any references or similarities to actual events, real people, living, or dead, or to real locales are intended to give the novel a sense of reality. Any similarity in other names, characters, places, and incidents is entirely coincidental.

Distributed by Kensington Publishing Corp.
Submit Wholesale Orders to:
Kensington Publishing Corp.
C/O Penguin Group (USA) Inc.
Attention: Order Processing
405 Murray Hill Parkway
East Rutherford, NJ 07073-2316
Phone: 1-800-526-0275
Fax: 1-800-227-9604

Acknowledgments

It is with pleasure that I am able to present to you what I consider to be one of my best works of drama to date. It has always been my desire to write stories that not only capture the interest of the readers through the drama, but to bring an understanding to many topics that affect our communities.

First I have to give much love and respect to my parents, Paul and Helen Long. Your love and support throughout my life is nothing but pure Love, and I thank God for allowing me to be your son and for you always putting up with me. Paul Long, Jr., my brother, thanks for ALWAYS having my back! Granny and Pop, thanks for the foundation and the beautiful love you've always shown. To Peyden and Kennedy, I appreciate you guys more than words can express! And know all I do, I do for you! Kristen Scott, thanks for all the support. We are definitely growing! Al and Tamala Boyd, thanks a million for the love and support! B.R. Wilson, man, you know we've been through hell and high waters together, and our friendship will always stand the test of time! Wade "Spoony G" Witherspoon III, your friendship is definitely GOLDEN! Josephine "Jo Dog" Dogan, thanks for everything and the opportunity you have given me with the store. Sandra Calhoun-White, thank you for all the support and encouragement you've given me! Jimiko "Miko Wiko" Witherspoon, thank you for still being my good "buddy." Terry and Christy Lewis, love you two with all my heart. Thanks for being family. The Gethsemane Church Family, thanks for the support, even though some of you say I write too nasty. (Ha Ha!) John Sutton, man, you know you my main dog! Thanks for the processing when it's needed. The Fellas: Bunny, Derrick, Mario, DeMario, Darren, Chuck, and Stacey, thanks for keeping me grounded.

To all the authors I've met and become close friends with over the years, I thank you much for all the advice and support given. Dwayne S. Joseph, words can never express my gratitude for all you've done. Your support has been wonderful! La Jill Hunt, thanks for all the encouragement you've given me. Sheila, you know you are nothing but a "Jewel." Thanks for all you've done and the wonderful friendship. D.L. Sparks, my literary twin, you're definitely about to show your glitter to the world! (LOL) Tina Brooks McKinney, my literary aunt, you have done so much, and I appreciate you dearly. Your love and support has definitely been a godsend. Nichole Payton, thanks for being my new literary friend, and I can't wait to pick up your first novel. You are definitely a gifted writer! Linda Herman, thanks for the friendship and allowing me to vent when needed! (LOL) Timmothy B. McCann, your encouraging words have blown me away, and I am honored that you've taken the time to read my work. Rosalyn McMillan, I'm truly honored for your comments on *The First Person*. You have truly inspired me to write from my heart. Eric Pete, thanks for being the writer that you are and giving me the challenge to up my game. I've come in contact with many authors over the years that in their own way influenced me. I thank each and every one of you for that.

Portia Cannon, I appreciate all you've done, as well as the patience you've shown me. Thanks a million!!!! To Carl Weber and the Urban Books family, again I thank you for this

Acknowledgments

opportunity, and I'm looking forward to a great relationship. Kim Floyd, I truly appreciate all you've done to help in supporting my career.

To all my MySpace and Facebook friends, thanks for all the love shown! Continue to keep that love flowing! To EVERYONE I have crossed paths with, for whatever reasons God has placed us in one another's lives, I'm sure it was for reasons for greatness to come from it. I love you all, even if your name doesn't appear!

Thanks, and I hope you enjoy!

Péron F. Long

Peron1@peronflong.com
www.peronflong.com
www.myspace.com/lilsouthernboy36

Prologue

Death appeared to have come too easily for him. It was almost as if he had gotten away with all of the evil he had placed on me. He didn't seem to suffer at all. I wanted him to suffer in the same manner in which I had for so long.

"Damn you!" I said aloud as I looked over his dead body. His eyes remained open, almost laughing at me. "Damn you!"

I walked through the dark woods, feeling more rage than when I began my journey earlier that morning. For some reason, I thought that the sun would suddenly jump out into the sky and give me the shine that I had been deprived of for so long.

As I arrived at my car, I stopped, turned slowly, and raised my eyes to look in the direction I had just traveled. I fell to the ground, my knees aching in pain as I slumped in prayer, hoping that somehow God would allow me to repent one more time for my already long list of indiscretions.

1

T'Shobi Wells

I looked over at the clock and suddenly became pissed that I had allowed myself to fall asleep. Justine was supposed to have been gone a long time ago. As a matter of fact, she wasn't supposed to be there at all.

Ordinarily, my rule was not to allow anyone who didn't call first into my humble abode, but for whatever reasons, I allowed her to get away with that rule far too many times; and regardless of how many times I reminded her, she still chose to do things in her own way.

When I got up from my bed, I heard the vibration of my phone going off for the umpteenth time. I didn't bother to look to see who it was. I already knew. My plans for the evening were drastically delayed, and there was no need to look at my missed calls or to listen to the voicemail messages that would only remind me of where I was supposed to be.

"Justine," I said as I gently nudged her. "It's almost twelve o'clock. You need to get up now. I'm sure Pastor Reynolds is wondering where his wife is."

"Fuck him," she mumbled. "His tired ass is probably somewhere with one of his *tricks*."

"Seriously, Justine, I don't think that it's cool for you to stay out so late. I'm almost certain that he's worried sick about you."

She finally began to move around under the sheets, while continuing to mumble curses. As I watched her naked body emerge from the bed, I noticed how perfect it was and the fact that at her age, with two adult children and three grandchildren, she remained so beautiful. Her honey-colored skin was immaculate, and her body could compete and win any day against any young woman in her early twenties.

I remembered the first day I met her. All I could think of was how much she reminded me of Phylicia Rashad. Yes, I can admit that when I was younger, I had a huge crush on Claire Huxtable.

In all of my twenty-seven years on this earth, I'd never dated or had sex with a woman my age or younger. I'd always been attracted to older women. Partly, I knew, it stemmed from the fact that my mother was never a major part of my life. I tried not to get into all the psychoanalytical bullshit, but I realized her giving me up at an early age and my once strong desire to find motherly love had a lot to do with it.

"I'm not sure if I like the fact of you kicking me out of your apartment, T'Shobi. This is the third time in a row," she said as she walked out of the bathroom. "I'm beginning to think that you and that damn Tinisha Jackson really are having a thing. Don't think that I don't hear the little rumors floating around the church."

I stood silently as she spoke. I had heard the rumors too, but that's all they were. Tinisha was five years younger than I was, and nowhere near my flavor of loving.

"Justine, you know those are just lies. Since coming to New Deliverance as the minister of music, there's only been one woman that I've been with, or even desired to be with."

I walked toward her, wrapped my arms around that perfect body of hers, and allowed my lips to touch hers.

"Uh-huh, and it better stay that way, too."

***

After walking Justine to her car, I ran back to my room and checked my cell phone. Sixteen missed calls, ten messages on my voicemail, and five text messages. Without checking, I already knew who it was, so I decided to take a long, hot shower before calling back to inform the caller that I was on the way.

While the hot water splashed across my body, I began to think of my life over the past seven months. I moved from Atlanta, Georgia to Charlotte, North Carolina hoping to escape my past, but as always, my ways never allowed me to get as far as I wanted to, or as far as I needed to.

Suddenly, I heard the voice of the woman I came to know as my MeeMa, speaking to me the day I left Montgomery, Alabama nine years earlier: *Baby, no matter how far you run away, you will never be able to run from yourself.* As much as I didn't want to admit it, she told me nothing but the truth.

My MeeMa was a wise old woman who took me in as her own when I was sixteen. She was the one that taught me how to live, and even love again, after all the bullshit I had experienced in my short years of living.

Immediately after stepping out of the bathroom, I heard my phone buzzing once again, informing me of how late I was.

"I'm about twenty minutes away," I said, then hung up without waiting for a response.

Driving in my car, I thought about the first time I met Justine Reynolds, the First Lady of New Deliverance Temple Church. She walked into Pastor Reynolds's office without knocking.

"I'm sorry, Seth. I didn't realize you were meeting with someone." Her voice was melodic, sounding as if she were singing.

"Sweetheart," he began as he rose from his desk, "please come in and allow me to introduce you to our possible new minister of music, T'Shobi Wells."

"Oh, this is the infamous Mr. Wells. I must tell you, I've heard nothing but great things about you. If all is true, I can't wait to see how you can turn our music ministry around."

As Pastor Reynolds and I continued discussing what my duties would be, as well as my compensation, Justine pranced around the office as if she were cleaning up and making sure everything was in place. It was difficult for me not to notice her, and I could tell that she was checking me out as well.

I've always had a gift of knowing when someone wanted to sex me. I've been a musician for churches as long as I knew how to talk, and for some reason, I was always a target for older women. I had my very first sexual encounter days before my thirteenth birthday, with a woman old enough to be my mother. As I got older, I learned how to decipher certain looks and innuendos, a gift that was also a dreaded curse.

After Pastor Reynolds and I completed our conversation, I decided to attend services the following Sunday and get a feel for how things were there, as well as a feel for his congregation.

Once I drove into the parking lot, the first person I noticed was Justine. She damn near broke a heel flagging me down to instruct me that I could park my car in front of the sign that read: MINISTER OF MUSIC.

As soon as I locked the door of my BMW, she placed her arm inside mine and escorted me toward the front door.

"I see playing keyboards has been good to you," she said, looking back, admiring my car.

"It's been a blessing."

"Well, I'm sure you will find it a blessing if you decide to rest your magic fingers here at New Deliverance." She then gave me the most sensuous smile; I could actually feel my southern region begin to move.

When we walked into the huge church, everyone looked toward her as she continued to escort me to the front of the church, where the musicians sat. From the jealous look of the keyboardist, who they had been using as an interim, I could tell he wanted to kick my ass. Justine quickly shooed him away as if he were a small child in the way.

"I can't wait to see what those magic hands can do," she said with a wink before taking her rightful seat in the front row.

After services that day, Pastor Reynolds invited me over to their house for dinner. As I sat at the table with their two grown sons and their wives and children, I could feel Justine's eyes piercing my skin. I did my best to avoid eye contact with her, but she made it impossible. Every time she spoke, her question or topic of conversation was directed at me.

As much as I tried not to notice her, I did. She was exactly the type of woman that had always turned me on. She was mature, yet had the energy of a teenager. Her hair was short and black, with just a hint of gray that made her look distinguished, and as I said before, she had the body that could make any man shout hallelujah.

For weeks after accepting the job, I pleaded with myself not to take things to a sexual level with her, but as all temptations seem to do, it took me over like a raging bull. One week, five days, twelve hours, and fifty-two minutes of trying to hold out from her had caved in.

When I arrived at the hotel, thoughts of what happened when I was in Atlanta replayed in my head. A situation exactly like this was why I left. I wanted to start fresh. I wanted to start new. I thought leaving Atlanta would do that for me, but as the months began to pass, I realized that it wasn't Atlanta that I had to run from; it was me that needed to change.

Riding on the elevator of The Blake Hotel in uptown Charlotte, my mind quickly traveled back to that first dinner at Pastor Seth and Justine Reynolds's home. She wasn't the only one checking me out that day. She wasn't the only one telling me with their eyes what they wanted to do to me or have me do to them.

"Why the fuck do I continue to do these things?" I softly asked myself as I stepped out of the elevator.

When I arrived at the room, I lightly tapped on the door.

"About damn time. What in hell took you so long?"

"I'm sorry. I got tied up with something," I said as we embraced.

"Tied up with something, or with someone? The rumor is that you and that li'l cute girl Tinisha Jackson have a thing going on."

"Seth, you should know better than anyone that Tinisha Jackson is definitely not my flavor," I responded to my pastor as we both fell onto the bed to make love until the early hours of the morning.

2

Justine Reynolds

"I can't believe he kicked me out his apartment to be with that damn *bitch*," I said, talking to myself aloud on my way home from T'Shobi's apartment. "Who in the hell does he think he is? I am old enough to be his mother. Hell, I have two sons older than him, and not only do I know the game, I know how to play it better than him. He can deny it all he wants to, but I can see how that little heifer watches him and clings to him at church."

I turned my radio on, trying to allow the smooth sounds of George Duke to soothe my mind, but it didn't work. The more and more I thought about the way he threw me out of his apartment, the angrier I became.

"It appears to me that he will have to learn the hard way, if he doesn't hurry and change his ways. Yes, he may have some good dick, but a crazy pussy can trump a good dick any day. And, first lady or not, my pussy can get crazy. Believe that," I said, concluding my tirade in my car as if I were talking to my best girlfriend.

When I finally made it home, just as expected, Seth wasn't there. He was never there. He was just another fool who thought he could play the game better than I could. Thirty years of marriage and the son-of-a-bitch still believed that his shit

didn't stink. The mighty Reverend Seth Carlton Reynolds
was too caught up in his mess to even realize that I knew
about all of the women he'd been with over the years.

Sometimes I wished I had never married his ass. When we
first started dating, while we were both still in high school, the
Negro was a whore, and things hadn't changed since. They
only got worse. My friends warned me about him, but because
he was my first—and at the time, my best lover—I just allowed
him to be him. I had realized from my own daddy's escapades
that regardless of what a man had at home, he would still stray
out into the street for some ass.

I stayed faithful to him throughout our courtship and remained that way until our twelfth year of marriage. Like I
said, I knew what he was doing, and I just played it off as a
man being a man, but then I caught him having sex with my
younger sister, a secret that I'd since chosen to keep for damn
near eighteen years. That was when I knew it was time for the
game to change.

Seth and I met shortly after my parents separated and my
mother, younger sister, and I moved to Charlotte to live with
my grandmother. The first few weeks there were like living in
pure hell. I couldn't understand a word that anyone was saying, and everything seemed so slow. Not only that, it was the
mid-seventies, and just the thought of leaving New York and
living down South was depressing all by its damned self.

"Just wait. You're going to love it here," I remembered my
mother telling me. "The Southern boys here are much more
settled."

Honestly, I couldn't understand how she could tell me
that with a straight face. Both she and my father were born
and raised in the South, and he sure as hell wasn't a settled
Southern boy. Daddy cheated on Mama with just about any

and everyone. I never knew if she suspected he was cheating and pretended that it wasn't going on, but I will always remember the day she caught him—or shall I say the day we caught him. It shocked the hell out of me to come home from church and see Sister Madeline Wilcox lying up in the bed, naked and fast asleep in Daddy's arms. In all my life, I had never seen my mother act the way she did that hot July afternoon. Two days later, we were on the Amtrak heading south to plant new roots.

I often wonder how catching my father in the act affected my outlook on marriage. Of course, when Seth and I got married, him cheating never crossed my mind. As Mama told me, the boys in the South were true Southern boys, and not only that, they were also good churchgoing boys.

Seth was the youngest son of Pastor Carlton Reynolds, the pastor of my grandmother's church. When I saw him, it was love at first sight. He was a tall, dark, and slender boy with a low cut and the blackest, most beautiful eyes I had ever seen. For me, he looked completely different from the other boys I had ever found attractive. He didn't have the huge afro that I thought I loved to see the boys wear, and his clothes, although still fashionable, weren't the loud colors that everyone was wearing then.

The very first Sunday I attended church, immediately after the benediction, I was right up on him, introducing myself. I think I scared the shit out of him, because he had started to drool when his mouth opened. My mother always told me that I was too aggressive, but hell, if you want something bad enough, then you go after it, and that's exactly what I did and continue to do.

I hated thinking about the past. I hated thinking about the shoulda-woulda-couldas. I hated being in a marriage that lasted all of this time, yet never went anywhere, and would never go a damn place further than where it was.

I even hated the affairs I'd had for the past eighteen years. Well, not all of them. My current beau, T'Shobi, was a lover like no other. From the first day I met him, I knew he was going to have to flow in my rivers—and could his ass flow!

The first day I met him, his grayish-blue eyes made my panties so moist that it almost drove me crazy. I had seen him on TV several times before on different awards shows, either performing or receiving some type of award for his music, but that was nothing compared to looking at that fine, tall, light caramel brother with the long, wavy hair in person.

I have to admit, the first time we had sex, he scared the hell out of me. He was so rough and hard. It was as if every stroke were a punishment.

"Baby . . . oh, baby . . . You hurting me," I remembered saying as tears literally fell from my eyes. "Please, not so rough."

After apologizing, he was gentle, but I'll be damned if he still didn't get rough from time to time. I'd almost come to like it, but due to the size of his member and the roughness that accompanied it, he could soon wear out a sister's pussy.

Before saying my prayers and hoping for God to forgive me yet again for my sins, I tried to call T'Shobi back to let him know that I made it home safely. The phone went directly to his voicemail.

"That motherfucker is with that li'l slut," I said as I slammed my phone onto the dresser. "Fool doesn't realize I heard the shit buzzing the entire time I was there."

I felt the tension rise in my temples. I was less than half a second from putting my clothes on and taking my ass right back to his place to kick both his and that damn Tinisha Jackson's ass.

"Me and that li'l bitch need to have a conversation," I said to myself as I attempted to allow sleep to take over my anger-filled body.

3

Tinisha Jackson

I couldn't believe what was staring at me in front of my face—First Lady Justine Reynolds passionately kissing T'Shobi outside of his apartment. I was hurt. The man I knew was a godsend was kissing my pastor's wife at twelve midnight.

Sitting in my car on the other side of the parking lot, I felt the tears falling from my eyes. I felt a rage that made me want to jump out and kill them both.

"How could he do this to me?" I said aloud through my tears.

When she drove away, I wanted to go and knock on his door to tell him that I saw him; to tell him that I forgave him, and that I still loved him. I wanted to show him that whatever she did with him, I could do it better. I wanted to let him know that whatever I did to push him toward her, I would correct it.

With my hands still shaking and my heart still beating fast, I made myself open my car door.

"You can do this," I whispered to myself. "You need to tell him how you feel."

When I finally got the courage to get out of my car and walk toward his building, I saw him running down the steps. He got into his car then quickly disappeared into the night.

***

Driving home, I still couldn't believe what I had just witnessed. I knew he had been sleeping around with someone; I just didn't know who that someone could have been. The shock of it all had begun to kill me softly.

When I arrived home around one that morning, my roommate, Trice, and her boyfriend were sitting on the couch, watching TV.

"Hey, girl, how was your date with T'Shobi?"

"We had a fight," I said as I swiftly made my way to my room.

"You want to talk about it?" she asked, standing up from the couch.

"No," I said as I walked to my room.

I had met Trice when I first moved to Charlotte two years earlier. At the time, she was working as a temp at the law firm where I worked as a paralegal. We weren't what you would call friends. We barely spoke to one another. Ours was just a situation for both of us to save money.

Lying on my bed, I began to think about the past several months. What had begun as a fantasy somewhere took flight into a full-fledged relationship with only me involved. I thought about how special I felt when I sent myself flowers to my job with a card attached, from him to me.

"It's over," I whispered as I forced myself to sleep.

4

T'Shobi

"You don't have to be shy," he said, patting his hand on the bed, gesturing for me to come sit beside him.

I remained at the door, looking at him nervously, not sure what to do.

"You know I won't hurt you, don't you?"

I nodded my head as I slowly made my way closer to him. Once I sat down, he slowly massaged my neck with his right hand.

"You are too young to be so tense. Relax, okay?" he said as he placed his left hand on me and then softly kissed my neck. "You are in good hands with me."

I suddenly began to feel aroused, a feeling that was overwhelming for me. Although I knew it was wrong, it felt too much like right.

After instructing me to take off my clothes, he then positioned me at the head of the bed and began kissing my chest, moving slowly down toward my member. The feeling continued to overwhelm my body, and in a matter of moments, I felt myself ready to explode.

"How does that feel?" he asked, his voice muffled. I was speechless. "How does it feel?" he asked again, this time demanding an answer; but I remained speechless. "Does it feel good?"

"Yes!" I yelled as I jumped up from the bed.

"Is everything okay?" Seth asked me as I looked toward him realizing that I had been dreaming.

"I'm fine," I said, slowly emerging from the bed and walking toward the bathroom.

Splashing my face with cold water, I was feeling livid from the recurring dream. I had managed to avoid it for years, but over the past several months, it had returned. The dream was always the same, and always ended with me jumping up from my slumber. It was of my first encounter with a man, when I was fifteen years old. It was the first time I thought that I had felt love from anyone.

I went back to the bed, where Seth was waiting with his arms open, inviting me into an embrace. I accepted it willingly, although I was very aware that for him it was only sex. I allowed his hug to give me the love that I often craved—one that only seemed to engulf me when I was with men.

I knew my childhood had a lot to do with these feelings, and it seemed that the more I tried to live what people call a "normal" life, the clearer it became that it was something I would probably never experience in my lifetime.

Suddenly, I began to feel rage, hurt, and disgust take over as it always did, and I broke free from his hold.

"Where are you going?" he asked with a look of confusion.

"Home," I responded, collecting my clothes off the floor.

"You know you don't have to go, don't you?"

"Seth," I said, as the feeling of false love continuously swept over me like a raging fire. "I . . . I have a nine o'clock appointment," I lied.

As if a burst of energy exploded inside of him, he quickly rose from the bed, came to me, and grabbed my hand.

"When can I see you again?" he asked as he pulled me closer to him.

"The next few days are hectic for me. Can I call you tomorrow?"

The look on his face told me that he was disappointed. He began to stare me down as if he were trying to read thoughts that I didn't even realize existed in my mind.

"You are seeing that girl, aren't you?" he asked as he released from our embrace and returned to his lying position on the bed.

"Seth, no, I'm not. I told you Tinisha's not my flavor."

"Then why can't I see you later today? You know you bring something out of me that I crave like a drug."

I stared into his strong and masculine face. Although he looked nothing like him, he reminded me of a man I used to know, the same man that often invaded my dreams—the same man that I thought showed me love for the first time in my life.

"Seth, I really can't stay," I said, knowing that I wished I could live in that moment forever. "But I promise I will call you tomorrow. Okay?"

As he rose to a sitting position on the bed, with his lips sticking out to show his disappointment, just as the man in my dream had done, he patted his hand on the bed in an attempt to lure me toward him.

"Well, since you have to leave, come over here and give me some of that 'Lord have mercy,' " he said seductively.

I walked toward him slowly, falling on all fours, moving my way to his member as if I were a cat on a prowl. With a sly and devious grin on his face, he spread his legs wide, making my way to his pleasure more accessible.

"Ah . . . Lord have mercy on me," he whispered as I pleased him.

When I arrived at my apartment, I noticed someone kneeling in front of the door as if they were praying. At first I couldn't make out who it was, and to be honest, it made me feel very uneasy. Walking closer, I recognized the person and became very puzzled as to how she even knew where I lived.

"Tinisha?" I began. "What are you doing here?"

"Masheeta lashamba. Masheeta lashamba," she replied, speaking in tongues, with her hands in the air and her eyes closed as she remained on her knees.

"Tinisha." I called her name again, this time grabbing her by her arm, attempting to get her to her feet. "What are you doing?"

After several moments of a slight struggle, she finally rose from her kneeling position then stood in front of me, looking directly into my eyes.

"I saw you last night."

Her words almost shattered me.

"You . . . you saw me where?" I asked, wondering if she had seen me at The Blake Hotel with Seth.

With hands back in the air, she began to shake them at me viciously. "Masheeta lashamba. Masheeta lashamba," she began again as she walked away from me and toward her car.

5

Justine

"Good morning," the trifling bastard said to me as he strolled into the house at 12:14 in the afternoon.

"Don't you mean good afternoon?" I asked with attitude, receiving no response from him.

He walked upstairs to his room. I remained in the kitchen, cooking as I always did on Saturdays, preparing for dinner with our entire family on the following day.

I often wondered if everyone saw Seth and me for what we really were: distant roommates, not the happy couple we portrayed ourselves to be on Sundays and a couple of days out of the week.

I was looking for a larger pot to put the freshly cleaned collard greens in when I heard Seth coming back down the stairs.

"I'm heading to the church for a few hours to handle some business."

And just like that, the motherfucker was gone.

"What do you mean, no?" I asked T'Shobi after he refused to see me.

Shortly after I finished cooking, I called him to see if he could spend some time with me that evening. I was in desperate need of some more of his loving, and I refused to take no for an answer—although it appeared that at this moment, I had no choice.

"After I practice with the choir this evening, I have to go to the studio to finish up on a project."

"Can't the studio wait?" I asked, just hoping he would change his mind.

"No, Justine, it can't wait. You know I have obligations outside of you. I have to pay the bills. I will see you tomorrow at church, okay?" Without a response from me, he hung up.

I began to feel anger once again, and for whatever reasons, that little bitch Tinisha Jackson ran through my mind.

"Me and that little bitch will definitely have to have a come-to-Jesus tomorrow at church," I said with pure evil in my heart.

6

Seth

"It's shocking to hear from you," Brandi said to me as she answered the phone.

"Why is it a shock?"

"Stop playing dumb, Seth," she began before a slight pause. "You only call me when your other playmates aren't around, or they're not pleasing your healthy appetite."

"Brandi, you know it's nothing like that. I've just been busy for the past couple of months. You know how my schedule is," I said, partially lying.

"Mm-hmm, right," she said with a chuckle. "So, I take it you are here in town?"

"Yeah, just for a minute. Have time to see me?"

"Have I ever told you no?" she asked seductively.

"No, ma'am, you haven't."

"And after driving an hour and a half, would you take no for an answer?"

"Probably not," I said, laughing.

I had met Brandi six years earlier, and like most of my latest desires, she was in her late twenties when we began our fling. Although sexy and desirable, she wanted more than I could offer her. She constantly insinuated wanting to become exclusive, but for many reasons, I knew that was impossible. I also knew the more I had to deal with her, the more I would have to pay on several ends.

Our meeting came at a time when I began using the Internet with hopes of finding discreet partners to help satisfy a sexual appetite that had been a part of my life since I realized that my penis could do more than urinate. She was quite different from my previous interests, but at the time, she fulfilled a desire I never knew I had.

"Seth, do you have to leave now? Can't you stay a little while longer?" she asked me as I stood in front of the mirror, straightening my tie.

"Brandi, I have to prepare myself for the morning," I said as I turned around to face her, placing a check in her hand.

She was almost as tall as me, and very slender. Her body was the color of a Hershey's Special Dark candy bar, and it amazed me how it was free from any blemishes or scars.

"I'm going to surprise you one day and show up at your church. I need to see who has stolen all of your time away from me," she said with an eerie giggle as she pulled her locks back and placed a rubber band around them to keep them in place.

"I thought that this was what would prevent you from showing up," I said, pointing to the check.

The thought of her doing that was something that was always a fear. Not just from her, but from any other fling from my past. For whatever reasons, I never feared that T'Shobi would expose our affair. Given the fact that he had a lot going for him as a national recording artist, I figured he never really had a desire for people to view him as a lover of men.

***

On my way back home, I began to feel that my trip to see Brandi was basically a waste of time and money. Although sexually she fulfilled me for a moment, that fulfillment lasted less than the time it took for me to get to her. My thoughts while with her continued to focus on my night before with T'Shobi. In the few months I'd known him, I had found myself having feelings for him that I never had with anyone in my life, not even Justine.

"What the hell is wrong with me?" I whispered to myself as I drove in silence. "You know this is not a natural thing."

Once I pulled into the driveway of my home, I remained in the car, thinking about him. The way he allowed me to hold him. The way he allowed me to kiss him. Everything seemed so perfect with him. The way he sexed me was a way that no one had ever done before. It was strange to me, yet at the same time, it felt more than wonderful.

"Dad, you okay?" my youngest son, Chase, said as he tapped on my car window, interrupting my thoughts.

"Son, I'm great. Just sitting here having my time with the Lord," I said as I emerged out of my car then walked into the house with him.

7

Tinisha

Most of my Saturdays consisted of the same thing: sitting at home for most of the day, doing absolutely nothing but washing clothes, watching TV, and daydreaming. The only difference this Saturday was what occurred in the morning at T'Shobi's apartment.

After witnessing the events from the night before, I initially wanted to go to my pastor to inform him that I saw his wife leaving T'Shobi's house at midnight, but I decided to wait. I knew that was information that I had to keep to myself, at least for the moment. Pastor Reynolds was a great man of God, and I was definitely not going to be the one to inform him that he was married to a devil.

The whole scene baffled me. I just couldn't understand why she would treat her husband that way, and I knew without a doubt that she had dug her claws into T'Shobi. I could see from the look in his eyes when he came home and saw me praying at his door that he was just an innocent being who got caught up in her wicked trap.

When I joined New Deliverance, something about her always unnerved me. In my opinion, she never fit the spiritual profile that a first lady should have. I always knew that she was nothing but pure trouble.

I admit that when God directed me to go to T'Shobi's house to pray, I protested. I didn't want him to think that I was some kind of lunatic, but I knew I had to obey the Word and get that demonic spirit away from the home of one of God's chosen.

As I sat in my room in silence, my phone began to sing. I immediately answered, already knowing who was calling because of the assigned ringtone, one of his songs.

"Hey, how are you?" I sang excitedly into the phone.

"What the hell is your problem?" T'Shobi responded with much attitude.

I was silent. For whatever reasons, I couldn't quite understand the anger he had in his voice.

"T'Shobi," I began nervously, "baby, what's wrong?"

Other than his heavy breathing, there was nothing but deadly silence.

"Do us both a favor and stay the fuck away from me," he said then immediately hung up.

The phone remained to my ear as the tears began to fall furiously down my face. I had never heard him use language like that before, and to be honest, I couldn't understand why. Knowing without doubt that it was God that led me there, I thought he would understand that and be happy and run into my arms.

I wanted to call back, but I knew that there was only one thing that I could do at that moment—something my mother taught me to do as a child.

"Oh, masheeta . . ." I screamed out as I began my prayer.

8

T'Shobi

I immediately hung up the phone. Although I knew that Tinisha heard anger in my voice, the reality was that for the most part, it was fear. All of my life I had to run away from my demons, and I had begun to get tired. My life was a mess, and the sad thing was that I was born into it. It wasn't one that I chose.

I never had what would be considered a normal childhood. I didn't grow up with a traditional family; hell, I didn't even grow up with a dysfunctional family. From the age of three until I was nine, I stayed with six different foster families, until I was adopted by a pastor and his wife. It was with them that my love for music and my gift for it had been discovered.

For the first year, staying with the Pratts was like a dream. At an early age, I thought my life was finally heading in the right direction. They had one grown daughter, who was married and lived in California. They were an older couple, in their late fifties, and initially they spoiled me to no end.

Mrs. Pratt was a music teacher at the local high school, and was the one that discovered my gift when she heard me playing the piano in their home. Every day for two hours we would sit at the piano and she would teach me how to read music and hone my skills.

One day when I was ten, my dream finally turned into a nightmare. Mrs. Pratt and I were sitting on the piano stool together when, without warning, she began to kiss me. It wasn't the normal peck that a mother would give her son. She actually forced her tongue into my mouth. That, at the time, I thought was the most disgusting thing in the world.

"Take your clothes off," she demanded.

"Hunh?" I responded, confused by her directive.

"I said take them off now."

Afraid, I followed her instructions. I thought I was being punished for something. In the past, the families I stayed with had been both mentally and physically abusive toward me, often for no reason at all, so although I was confused, this wasn't anything new.

She examined me as I stood in front of her naked. She then instructed me to come closer to her as she removed her dress. This was new. It was the first time I had seen a naked woman, and it was so nasty that I felt like I wanted to vomit.

Mrs. Pratt was a very dark, large, and unattractive woman, and wore a wig every single day, even if she never left the house. She had a huge mole on her chin that had one string of hair growing from it. Each of her breasts were as large as my head, and she had a forest of hair living under her arms.

"It's time that we make you a man," she said as she began to fondle my penis.

This abuse went on for almost three years, every day, even that time of the month when she had to go through her *situation*.

Then one day, as if I hadn't already been through enough, Reverend Pratt came home early from work to see me on top of his wife, servicing her. She immediately cried rape, and I was sent to a juvenile sex offender treatment facility four hundred miles away from Alabama.

After staying at the facility for nine months, I was released and returned to Alabama, where I was forbidden to come in contact with the Pratts.

For three months, I stayed at a group home, until I was rescued by Ms. Robbie Mae Talford. Ms. Talford, who I called MeeMa, was my new savior and a woman I loved with all I had. For almost two years, it was just MeeMa and me, until her son, Russell, came home from prison.

My phone began to sing the assigned melody as I drifted out of my dreadful past that reminded me I was currently living in a dreadful present.

"What are you doing?"

"Just sitting here listening to what I recorded tonight in the studio," I replied.

"It's still early. Are you going to meet me?"

"Give me an hour," I replied without a second thought.

9

Justine

It was 10:30 when I left my house on my way to see T'Shobi. I was happy that he finally decided to see me. After calling him a thousand times, while Seth had gone to wherever the hell it was he went to when he left our house earlier, he finally caved in and told me that I could come over.

"Where are you going this time of night?" Seth asked as I placed my purse around my shoulders and retrieved my keys.

"Out. I will be back shortly."

You didn't answer my question," he said with a strong attitude.

"Where the hell have you been all day?"

He remained quiet.

"Just as I thought," I responded as I walked out of the door with no more words.

It was no secret to him that I had my affairs, and there was not a damn thing he could do about them. That was something that was established a long time ago. He knew I was more than aware of his indiscretions, and although we never talked about them, it was just something that was somehow understood between us.

***

When I arrived at T'Shobi's apartment, I almost choked from the smoke. "I thought you stopped smoking that stuff," I said, disappointed at his use of marijuana.

"Had a long and stressful day. I needed something to relax me."

"Well, I thought that's why you invited me over—to relax you," I said as I walked toward the couch and sat beside him.

"How do you know you are not one of my stresses?" he asked with a smirk on his face.

I didn't know if he was serious or joking, but in the months that I had known him, he'd always been somewhat distant. Some days were better than others, but for the most part, he was hard to crack.

He never went into a lot of details about his past; however, he told me enough to let me know that he had a difficult childhood. When he explained to me about all of the foster homes he had been to and how he was once sent away to a facility for a juvenile offense as a child, I thought about how blessed my childhood really was, and how blessed my children were, even though they had two parents who did some not so positive things in their lives.

"So, how was your day?" I asked, trying to change the atmosphere of the room.

"Like any other day."

There was a cold silence between the two of us as he inhaled the burning brown leaf that hung from his mouth.

"Can you please put that out? I don't want to go home smelling like that," I demanded.

"You asked to come here, so deal with it."

I decided to leave him on his couch as I made my way to his bedroom, where I remained on his bed naked for twenty-five minutes before he decided to come and grace me with his presence.

He stood over me, staring at me with those hypnotizing eyes as he slowly began to remove his clothes. Looking at his chiseled body made all of me melt. I wanted him desperately.

Once he removed his jeans and underpants, I opened my legs so that he could do with me as he pleased. His eyes never looked away from me as he dropped to the floor on his knees to please me with his tongue.

"Damn, baby, that feels good," I moaned with pleasure. "Shit, that feels so good."

He rose from the floor, grabbing both of my legs, and pulled me closer to the edge of the bed. With a thunderous force, he rammed all of him into my waiting, willing, and oh so wet pussy.

"Fuck!" I yelled. It was painful, yet at the same time, pleasurable.

"You cried all day about getting this dick. You acting like you scared now."

"No, baby, it feels good," I said through the pain. "Please give me all you have."

After hearing that, he did something to me that made me quickly regret those words.

"Turn over and get on all fours," he demanded, and I did what he told me to do. "You sure you can handle all I have?"

"Yes," I moaned with anticipation.

Before I knew anything, he brought my ass closer to him, and with all his force, rammed the head of his dick directly into my rectum. After screaming for what seemed like an eternity, I quickly jumped off the bed.

"T'Shobi, what the hell is wrong with you?"

"You told me to give you all I had," he said with a devilish smirk.

"You know you can't just ram your dick in my ass," I said as I began gathering my clothes off the floor.

"I'm not done."

"Nigga, your ass is done tonight," I responded.

Suddenly, a look I had never seen flashed across his face. It was a look that seriously scared the hell out of me.

"Justine, I said I was not done."

I stared at him, hoping to find some type of emotion from him outside of what I was actually seeing. "You are high," I said.

"Yes, I am, and your point?"

"I need to go home." I had become even more frightened by his behavior. Although he had been a bit rough in the past, this was the first time he had attempted to have anal sex. Now, I was not totally against it; however, it was the way he went about it, no warning or anything.

"Okay, since you're ready to go home, let's make a deal."

"I'm listening."

"You go home now, without me finishing, and you never come back again."

Once again, those grayish-blue eyes stared at me long and hard, giving me no indication if what he was saying was fact or fiction.

"You have any K-Y?" I asked.

"No."

"Damn. Well, go get some Vaseline or something. That shit hurts," I responded as I dropped my clothes to the floor and reassumed my position on the bed.

10

Seth

I arrived at the church around seven in the morning with the hopes of finding some much-needed time of peace and solitude. The night before was extremely restless, and several thoughts continued to dance in my head.

Usually when Justine left the house, it didn't bother me; however, for some reason, this particular time touched a nerve that I couldn't quite explain.

I was sitting in my office upstairs when she arrived home at three A.M. From the way she walked into the house, I could tell she didn't know if I was asleep or not. She was making an extra amount of noise, which informed me that she didn't really care if she had awakened me.

"It's kind of late for you to be coming in, isn't it?" I asked

"Hmph, at least I do come home," she mumbled as she walked to the room that we once shared years ago.

"Justine, where have you been?" I asked.

"Go to hell, Seth." She slammed the door.

I rose from my desk, trying to understand why, that night, unlike any before, I even cared about where she had been or who she had been with.

I knew that I would get no answers from her, so I decided to go my designated bedroom, our son's old room, and attempt to get some sleep.

Lying in the bed, once again I thought about T'Shobi and
how I had begun to have strong feelings for him. Then suddenly, Brandi became a thought, and my eyes never closed to
help my body obtain the much-needed sleep it required.

"Pastor Reynolds, you here mighty early," Deacon Barber said as he walked into my office, breaking me out of my
thoughts. "I wasn't expecting you here for another hour or
so."

"I came in a little early to convey with Lord, Deacon Barber," I said, once again using the Lord, as I had so many times
in the past, as an excuse for my sinful ways.

"Well, I won't disturb you. You be blessed." As quickly as
he came in, he left.

Again, those thoughts of T'Shobi and Brandi began to
play in my head, causing a slight headache. I couldn't grasp
my feelings, but for whatever reasons, I was beginning to feel
something strange brewing.

11

Tinisha

"Praise the Lord, my sanctified daughter!" my mother sang into the phone before I could say hello.

"Praise the Lord. Good morning, Mama."

"Baby, you sound like you still in bed. It's almost seven. You should have been up two hours ago in prayer. Are you sick?"

From the day I began talking, my mother had instilled in me to wake up and pray every morning at five. It was something that was mandatory, and there were no excuses for anyone in her house, with the exception of my father, not to follow that rule.

"Mama, I've been up. I just laid down for a few moments before going to church."

"Well, baby, today is the Lord's day, and you have to get up and go praise Him. You don't have time to lay back down. You have souls to go save. Now, I'm not going to hold you up, so get up and go about the Lord's business. Be blessed, and call me this evening." She hung up before I could say anything.

Although my mother and I lived more than a hundred miles apart, I obeyed her as if I were still in her home.

Standing in the shower, my thoughts went back to my conversation the night before with T'Shobi. He was mad at me, and to be honest, I was frightened to go to church and have to face him. The sound in his voice led me to believe that if he had been close by, he could have possibly done some physical harm to me.

Before leaving for church, I decided that since I missed my five A.M. prayer, I should at least try to get a quick one in before walking out the door. Mama told me a long time ago that if I ever left anywhere before praying for a safe arrival, God was not pleased and harm would come to me. Regardless if I was just going outside to my mailbox, or leaving to go on an extensive drive, I prayed, not wanting to take any chances.

When I arrived at the church, I looked toward T'Shobi's designated parking spot to ensure he hadn't arrived yet; then I darted inside. I wasn't sure how he was going to react, and to be honest, I was even more afraid than I had been earlier that morning of what he may say or do.

"Good morning, Sister Jackson," Pastor Reynolds said, nearly scaring me to death with his sudden appearance.

"God bless. Good morning, Pastor Reynolds."

He stared at me for a very long time, as if he were trying to read my thoughts. It was kind of weird to me, because he had never really given me so much as a slight glance since I began attending the church.

"How are things going with you?"

I remained speechless, not sure how to answer his question. It almost felt as if he knew that I had something to tell him. I wondered if this was a sign from God, informing me to let Pastor Reynolds know about his wife and T'Shobi.

"Everything is well, Pastor. Thanks for asking."

As he walked away, I touched his arm as if I had more to say.

"Yes, Sister, is there a problem?"

I stood frozen, with my heart thumping as if it were going to jump out of my chest and run away. "Uhh . . . errr . . . Pastor, there . . . is something . . ."

Before I could utter another word, T'Shobi appeared out of thin air.

"Everything is fine, Pastor Reynolds," I quickly spat out as I walked in the opposite direction of them.

After that small amount of time around T'Shobi, I was so scared that I left church, choosing not to stay for Sunday school, much less for the service that followed it.

12

T'Shobi

After Justine left my apartment, I finished smoking what was left in the little plastic bag. I wasn't what you would call a weed head; it wasn't something that I did very often, but I was trying my best to leave the world I was in, even if only for a moment.

As I inhaled, I thought about what had just taken place in my bed. In a sense, it could be said that I had just committed rape. It was the first time that I ever considered myself a rapist, even given the fact that I was once labeled a sex offender.

When I forced myself into Justine, her initial reaction was what I was hoping for so that I could give her an ultimatum. It was an ultimatum she was supposed to accept, but instead, my plan backfired on me.

"Next time, give me a warning first," were the last words she said to me as she walked out the door.

My life was more complicated than I could handle. I couldn't understand why God saw fit for me to live, much less prosper, in the way I had for so many years. When I was seventeen and began to elevate in the music industry, I thought that maybe this was God's way of paying me back for all the hell He had allowed in my life at such an early age. But ten years later, my struggles were still present. I had money, a successful career, and my name known by many, but there were still several things missing in my life that I knew would never come. Since leaving Montgomery, I had never stayed in a city more than two years, and as quietly as I entered new cities, I left them.

To my surprise, I arrived at the church early. I wanted to call Seth and tell him that I wasn't going to be there. Not only was I nervous to see Justine after what had just happened, I was terrified to see Tinisha. I honestly didn't know what to expect from her.

As I turned the corner and saw Tinisha and Seth in a conversation, I considered running out of the church and back into my car. I would drive nonstop to Montgomery, forgetting that I had ever known where Charlotte, North Carolina was.

Before I could turn around, my eyes locked in on Tinisha. She had a look of fear in her eyes, and before I knew it, she was gone.

"Good morning, Pastor Reynolds," I said, attempting to be professional.

"Good morning, Brother Wells. God bless," he responded in the same professional manner before walking toward the entrance to the church.

I decided to try to catch Tinisha before services started, to apologize for my outburst. I was still mad as hell, but at the same time, I needed things to be smooth with her, due to not knowing exactly what it was that she saw or who she saw me with.

I walked in the direction she went, but didn't see her anywhere. When I walked out to the parking lot, I saw her car leaving, and again I became nervous, not knowing what to expect.

***

Church service that morning went as normal as ever, and the only thing that I noticed different was that Justine was not there. Although relieved, I wondered if my actions the night before caused her any pain. I couldn't help but admit that I was rough with her. It was as if all of the anger in my body raged out of me all at once. I was hurting, and I wanted someone to feel the same way that I did; although I knew that was highly impossible. No one could ever understand my pain unless they actually experienced life the way I had.

As I was walking out of the church, a young man with neat locks and smooth, flawless dark skin, wearing jeans and a brown sport coat that appeared almost too big, approached me.

"I'm a huge fan of your music," he said with his hand extended for me to shake.

"Thanks. I really appreciate that." I attempted to walk away, but he refused to let my hand go.

I began to study him, noticing several feminine qualities. I stayed away from guys like him, the overly flamboyant gay men, as much as possible. I never knew if it was my occupation that set off their radar and attracted them to me.

"Would you like to have dinner with me?" he asked.

"Thanks for the offer, but I have plans."

"So do I," he responded with a sly smirk as he released my hand slowly and walked away.

Less than two seconds later, Seth was standing at my heels, staring at me for what seemed like an eternity.

"Do you know him?" he asked with a strong look of concern on his face.

"No, I don't."

"Well, I do, and I strongly suggest that you stay away from

him. He's a very dangerous individual," Seth said as he vanished back into the church.

When I finally arrived at my car, I noticed that the guy who I was just warned about was standing by a red Porsche Cayenne, staring at me before getting into the expensive SUV.

"What was that all about?" I asked myself as I retrieved my phone to call Tinisha. As much as I wanted to avoid her, I knew that a conversation with her would have to take place soon.

"Tinisha," I began when she answered after the first ring. "Can we meet somewhere and have dinner and talk?"

She was silent for a moment. I could tell even over the phone that she was timid about meeting me.

"I'm not angry with you, Tinisha. I just believe that you and I really need to converse about some things."

Before I could utter another word, she quickly agreed, even choosing the restaurant where we would meet.

13

Justine

It was noon when I decided to get out of the bed. After arriving home from T'Shobi's apartment, I took a long bath, soaking my aching bottom in warm water, looking for some type of relief. Not only was my body still in pain from his roughness, my heart was hurting also.

Although I tried to convince myself that I wasn't, I was actually falling in love with him, and that, I already knew, was a no-no.

After my bath, I lay in bed and remained there for the entire morning, staring at the ceiling. I wanted to get up, but my heart, along with my hurting ass, would not allow any other part of my body to do anything but lay in bed with tears falling from my eyes.

After what seemed like an eternity, I finally forced myself up. I knew that I had to leave before Seth came home. Sundays were family day, and this was not a day I wanted to be around my children or grandchildren. And I sure as hell didn't want to see Seth.

I dressed then walked downstairs and left a note, telling them to eat dinner without me. I got into my car and began driving with no set destination. I drove around Charlotte aimlessly, as if gas wasn't near ten dollars a damn gallon. My phone constantly chimed, letting me know that someone was looking for me, but I didn't bother to look to see who was calling.

I was so deep into my thoughts that it took me a moment to realize that my stomach was calling for me to get something to eat. I decided to drive to the uptown area to eat at Addie's, one of my favorite Jamaican restaurants. As I searched for a parking place on the street in front of the restaurant, I noticed T'Shobi's car leaving, and I saw Tinisha following directly behind him in her piece of shit Ford.

"Motherfuckers!" I screamed as I made a sudden stop. Without realizing there was a car directly behind me, I jumped out of mine. The last thing I remembered hearing was a horn blowing before a loud crash.

14

Tinisha

"Yadda moshamba masheeta lashamba. Yadda moshamba masheeta lashamba."

"Tinisha, you need to calm down," I heard T'Shobi say as I continued praying.

"Yadda moshamba masheeta lasham. Ba, yadda moshamba masheeta lashamba"

"Tinisha," he yelled. "Calm down!"

I was a nervous wreck. When I turned onto to Davidson Street, I heard a loud crash. When I looked back to see what had happened, I was in complete shock at not only what I saw, but who I saw.

"Call nine-one-one," T'Shobi instructed as he ran toward the car that had been hit.

I was motionless. I couldn't believe what I was seeing: First Lady Justine Reynolds, face down on the ground and motionless.

"I couldn't avoid her," said the short, balding white man who was driving the car that hit her. "She stopped so quickly there was nothing I could do."

"Tinisha, don't just stand there. Call nine-one-one," T'Shobi instructed again.

I remained in the same spot for several moments, not moving. The thoughts that began to play in my head were so evil that I knew I was going to have to go into serious prayer for even thinking them.

"Yes, there's been an accident," I told the operator reluctantly.

Once EMS placed her in the ambulance, I returned to my car, hoping that T'Shobi would do the same. Instead, I saw him get into the back with her, never once looking toward me.

"I should have let the bitch die," I said, feeling not the least bit of remorse.

15

Seth

"What are you doing here?"

Immediately after church, I confronted Brandon, and demanded that he meet with me in my office.

"I came to be spiritually fed," he said, sitting in front of me with a smirk on his face.

"I told you never to come here."

"Seth, I thought everyone was welcomed into the house of the Lord." He crossed his legs and stared directly into my eyes.

I returned his glare, hoping that he didn't see the nervousness that raged in my body.

"So, tell me, what's the deal with you and your musician?"

"What do you mean?" My eyes darted away from him.

"Just as I thought. Seth, you are definitely one of a kind."

"You still didn't tell me why you came here today."

"As I stated earlier, I came to be spiritually fed." He rose from the chair and began to walk toward the door. "May God be with you and your family," he said then left.

"Pastor Reynolds, you have a call on line two from Brother Wells," my secretary informed me.

I felt my heart begin to smile. It was something strange

about T'Shobi. Just the mere thought of him, or hearing his name, made me feel good inside, regardless of what was going on at the time.

He had been constantly on my mind, and I was hoping to hear from him after church, especially after the conversation that I had just had with Brandon.

"You were just on my mind, Mr. Wells."

"Seth, you have to come to Carolinas Medical immediately!"

"What's wrong? Are you okay?"

"There's been an accident."

"T'Shobi, are you okay? What happened?"

"Justine was just in a very bad accident. Things aren't looking good."

God may not forgive me, but after he said Justine was hurt and not him, I was relieved.

When I arrived at the emergency room and saw T'Shobi and Tinisha sitting in the waiting room together, I felt a strong sense of jealousy engulf my body.

"What happened?" I asked T'Shobi suspiciously.

On my way to the hospital, my thoughts were bombarded with how T'Shobi knew about Justine's accident before me.

"Se—Pastor Reynolds, I'm really not sure. As Tinisha and I were leaving Addie's restaurant, we heard a loud crash. When I looked back, I recognized Justine's car, and I immediately ran to assist."

"You two had dinner together?" I asked, looking at him and then her, then back at him again. I couldn't believe how seeing the two of them together, and now discovering that they had dinner together, concerned me more than my wife being in an accident.

"Yes," T'Shobi said softly.

"Pastor Reynolds, your wife will definitely be in my prayers," Tinisha said as she came closer to give me a hug.

While in our embrace, I glanced over at T'Shobi, giving him a look of disgust to let him know that I knew he had lied to me about his involvement with Tinisha. His eyes never looked my way, remaining focused on the ground.

"You may want to inform them that you are here," he finally said.

Without any words, I walked to the front desk of the ER. As I stood at the desk, waiting to be acknowledged, I looked back to where the two of them were sitting. He said something to her, and then she left.

"Is your little girlfriend leaving?" I asked once returning to where he was sitting.

"Seth, she is not my girlfriend. How many times do I have to tell you that she's not my type?"

His expression and tone seemed believable, but the jealousy had taken so much control, I refused to believe him. We remained silent until the receptionist called my name to inform me that the doctor was ready to see me.

Again, my thoughts of concern never steered toward my wife.

"Hello, Mr. Reynolds. I am Dr. Carlisle," a tall and young-looking white man said to me as he extended his hand for me to shake. "Your wife is currently in a coma. Honestly, the injuries she's sustained could have easily killed her, but she appears to be a very strong woman who refused to die." He paused for a few moments then directed me through a set of double doors to go and see her.

As we walked through the doors, I looked back at T'Shobi and noticed he was walking out of the ER. I wondered where he was going and if he would be there when I returned.

The doctor and I arrived at the room where Justine was. All I saw was a bandaged woman that slightly resembled my wife connected to a bunch of tubes.

"As I stated," Dr. Carlisle began, "she appears to be a very strong woman."

I stared at her long and hard, feeling no sense of sadness. I had no concern for her state of being. My eyes just remained on this shell of a woman I used to pretend to love.

Once I returned to the lobby of the ER, I scanned the room, looking for T'Shobi, but the only familiar faces I saw were my two sons and their wives. After I shared with them what Dr. Carlisle told me, they took turns visiting their mother. Becoming restless, I decided to step outside to make a phone call.

"Why are you not answering your phone?" I asked on T'Shobi's voicemail.

16

T'Shobi

On the drive back to my car, Tinisha attempted to talk to
me, but her words were ignored. I couldn't explain it, but I
was feeling guilty for a number of reasons.

At the hospital, when I saw Seth rush in, I felt the weight of
a thousand hands pressing down on my chest. I began questioning myself and the decisions I'd made. I didn't understand why I allowed myself to have an affair with both him
and his wife. And because of my affair with his wife, she was
lying in a hospital emergency room near death.

"I saw First Lady Reynolds leaving your apartment Friday
night," Tinisha spoke softly, saying the first thing I actually
heard since getting into the car. "That's why I was at your
steps, praying her demonic spirit away yesterday morning."

I remained silent, looking out of the window. I didn't want
to face her at that moment, although in all honesty, I was
relieved by what she said. Surprisingly, since the moment she
revealed that she had seen me, it hadn't occurred to me that
she meant seeing me and Justine together. I was almost certain that she had found out about me and Seth.

"How long have you and her been . . . been sinning?"

I remained silent.

***

When we arrived back at my car at the restaurant, I immediately exited her car, never looking back. As I was about to
enter mine, Tinisha leaned out of the window.

"Pastor Reynolds is a great man of God." She paused, and
I could feel her staring at me. "Do you love her?"

My response was closing my door, turning the key in the
ignition, and driving away. Looking back in my rearview mirror, I noticed she had stepped out of her vehicle and fell to
her knees, raising her arms in the air. I assumed she was doing what I'd seen and heard her do several times in the past
several hours—pray.

The next morning, I woke up later than normal. My body
was aching, and my mind was still in a complete daze. I had
hoped that the events of the night before were only a bad
dream; however, the ringtone of my phone reminded me that
sleep was my only peace, and my only moments of solitude
from my daily hell.

"Good morning, Seth," I said groggily into the phone.

"Justine is still in a coma."

"Are you at the hospital?" I asked.

"No. I came home around two o'clock this morning."

There was a long pause. I didn't know what to say to him. I
wanted to tell him that I was leaving town never to return, but
at the same time, I wanted him to hold me in his arms the way
he had done in the past during our times together. It was hard
to explain, but all of my adult life, the only time I had ever
been able to find the feeling of love was in the arms of a man.

"Can we see each other today? I really need to see you," he
said.

"I'm just waking up and already late for my first session in
the studio."

There was another long pause. I knew he had questions; the kind that I had no definite answers to.

"Will you call me later?"

"Yes, Seth, I will," I said then hit the end button before any other words could be said by either one of us.

"Shobi, this track is hot! I love the concept. I have the perfect lyrics for it."

Al Boyd was an artist I had been working with since coming to Charlotte. The first time I heard him sing, I was mesmerized. I had always dreamed of working with him one day. When I was twelve, he was part of an R&B band that had one hit that raced up the charts, then suddenly, they were never heard from again—until now.

"Thanks. I appreciate that," I responded nonchalantly.

"Yo, man, is everything okay?" he asked.

My eyes never left the soundboard, and I began nervously touching buttons as if I were actually working.

"Earth to T'Shobi," he said, laughing.

"Sorry, Al. I've just had a horrible past few days," I said as I stood up from my stool, walked out of the sound booth, and into the room beside it that I used as an office.

I grabbed a bottle of water out of the small refrigerator beside my desk and stood by the window, looking out at nothing.

"Not trying to pry all up in your business," Al began as he walked into the office, "but the past few studio sessions we've had, you've been, like, in a trance. You sure everything is cool?"

My mouth wanted to tell someone my entire life story, but my mind knew better. My life was too much of a living hell to discuss with anyone, and half of what happened in my life was so unbelievable that sometimes I thought I had made it up.

"Relationship problems," I said solemnly, hoping that those two words would sum up my current state and answer all questions that he may have had.

"Trust me, man, I know what you talking about," he said, laughing before returning to the soundboard and replaying the track.

That evening after leaving the studio, I decided to stop by the hospital to check on Justine. She had been on my mind the entire day, and the feelings of guilt I had about her being in her current state had increased tremendously.

As I stepped off of the elevator onto the fifth floor, I damn near ran into the gentleman I had met at church the previous day.

"Oh, Mr. Wells, it's so good to see you again, and so soon," he said with a strange chuckle as he lightly tapped my chest with his hand.

"You too, Mr. . . . ?"

"Brandon. Brandon Myles," he said.

"Nice seeing you again, Mr. Myles," I said as I extended my hand to him.

He held my hand longer than I desired as he stared hard into my eyes with an eerie smile on his face. "Isn't it a shame what happened to First Lady Reynolds?" he asked, still providing that smile that was quickly making me want to knock the shit out of him.

I didn't know if Seth's comment about him being a dangerous individual was somewhere in the back of my mind or what, but something about Brandon Myles unnerved me. I mumbled something as I jerked my hand away from his and walked toward Justine's room.

"Hope to see you again in the very near future, Mr. Wells," he sang as I walked away.

17

Tinisha

It was exactly 5:45 on Monday morning when I began my daily hour of prayer. The first thing I prayed to God for was to forgive me for the evil thoughts that danced around my mind for Justine Reynolds to die. I knew when I was thinking them He wasn't pleased with me, but she had stolen what He had provided for me, and for that alone, I believed she should have been punished.

The night before, when I arrived home from taking T'Shobi to get his car, my roommate, as always, was sitting in the living room, watching TV with her boyfriend. I had no idea what was going on in my head at the time, but just seeing the two of them, his arms wrapped around her, made me snap.

"Why in hell do you always have to be over here?" I yelled at the top of my lungs. "I know at some point you two have to get sick and fuckin' tired of seeing each other!"

My roommate stared at me in total disbelief. I could tell by the way her lips began moving that she wanted to say something, but, unsure of my state of mind, she quickly gave any conversation with me a second thought.

I stood in front of them, hoping that someone said something to me. I don't know exactly what I would have done if they had, but I knew I was ready for something.

She slowly emerged from the couch, grabbing her man by the hand, and quietly, they both walked by me and went into her room. I remained standing in the living room, still heated and angry about all that had taken place a few hours earlier. I stood feeling nothing but pure rage.

I walked to my room, and the first thing I noticed were the flowers I had sent to myself days earlier. Without reservation, I picked up the vase and threw it to the other side of the room.

I heard mumbles coming from her room, but the only thing I could make out was "crazy bitch" coming out of the mouth of the only man in the apartment.

"You damn right! I am a crazy bitch," I yelled, not sure where all this new rage was coming from.

As much as it scared me, it also felt good. I had never used such language before, and I could honestly say that I had never remembered having those types of emotions before. After calming down, I took a shower then lay down, hoping that this emotion would finally leave, but at the same time wishing it would stay to help me do what needed to be done.

18

Justine

I slowly opened my eyes, unaware of where I was. I could feel the presence of another person near me, yet when I focused on the person sharing space with me, I had no idea who it was.

"Where am I?" I asked, but received no answer.

The mysterious person stared at me with a strange smile then walked out of the room. I looked around frantically, hoping to find some kind of familiarity, but nothing. Suddenly, after realizing I was in the hospital, everything came rushing to my mind on what had happened.

I suddenly became angry all over again; then, as if he appeared from thin air, I noticed T'Shobi walk in.

He stared at me long, and I noticed tears were falling from his eyes.

"Justine . . ." he said softly.

He remained with me for moments with no words, before slipping away just as quickly as he had arrived.

19

Seth

"Why was she on the other side of Charlotte?" my oldest son, Frederick, asked.

"I don't know."

"Why was T'Shobi there?" He asked the second question with grave curiosity. It was another question that not only was I unable to answer, but one that had constantly visited my thoughts over the past few days as well.

Two days after Justine's accident, I made several attempts to contact T'Shobi, but he never returned my calls. I even showed up at the Tuesday night choir practice, hoping to get a chance to talk with him, but he wasn't there. All of the choir members that showed up that night were informed once they arrived that practice had been canceled, but no one had actually spoken with him or had seen him.

As I was leaving the church, I noticed Tinisha walking toward her car.

"Sister Johnson . . ." I paused for a few moments, staring into her eyes, hoping to read any expressions she may have had. "Have you spoken with Brother Wells today?"

"No, Pastor Reynolds, I haven't spoken to him since Sunday," she said nonchalantly then walked to her car, leaving without so much as a care or concern.

"Did you and Mom have a fight?" My son continued drilling me with questions, breaking me out of my daze.

"Errr . . . No, son, we didn't. I left for church earlier than normal, and assumed your mother would arrive before services as she always did."

"Pops, things just seem strange to me," he said, pausing to sip the bottle of water he had retrieved from the refrigerator. "Have you been to see her today?"

"I was there earlier," I said, lying to my son. Truth was I hadn't visited my wife since the day of her accident. A part of me didn't care to, and that made me angry. I realized that it didn't make a lot of sense that we had been married for thirty years without an ounce of concern for each other. For years, I pretended that I loved Justine, when in reality, I never had so much as a like for her.

When my son left the house, I walked into my study and sat at my desk. Although I wasn't a heavy drinker, I knew with all that was going on within my own mind, I needed something to relax me. I opened the bottom drawer of my desk and pulled out the bottle of Courvoisier that I stored there. After pouring a decent amount into a glass, thoughts of my entire life began to play in my mind as if it were a Tyler Perry movie.

Justine and I had known each other since we were fifteen, and in all those years, we still didn't know a thing about one another. We never even took the time to get to know each other.

When we first met, although it was her who I became involved with and eventually married, it was her younger sister that I desired. From our first time meeting, Justine pursued me vigorously. Even when I showed that I had no interest in her, she continued to come after me. My father, who was the pastor of the church at the time, and who had been good friends with her grandmother, began to push us into a relationship, even when I stressed to him that I had no interest in her.

"Boy, that's a good girl who comes from good people," he told me. "She is the kind of young lady that you grow with. I know you have your preferences, but, son, it's time you realize the differences between the things you want and the things you need."

His words from so many years ago still played in my head as if it were just the day before. I never had a real talk with him about my desires, yet after that conversation, I honestly think he knew that I was always different.

After I poured another glass of Courvoisier, my cell phone rang. I looked on the display to see who was calling and was disappointed.

"How can I help you?" I asked, aggravated with the caller.

"I'm sure you already know the answer to that."

There was a long and silent pause.

"I'm at the Comfort Inn Suites by the airport. Room three-ten," the caller said before hanging up with no other words.

20

T'Shobi

For an entire week I sat on the floor of my dark apartment, drinking and smoking weed, trying desperately to rid myself of this crazy life I lived. Thoughts of my past continued to flow through my mind, and I wanted desperately for my life to end.

I didn't know what to do. The more I drank and the more I smoked, the more my past seeped out into my present, rearing its ugly head. Twenty-seven years of pain and disappointment all rushed down on me in five days.

In that five-day period, I envisioned myself killing my adoptive mother, Mrs. Pratt, several times for all she had done to me. Not only had she stolen my innocence, but she also stole any form of a life I could have had when she molested me and had me sent away and labeled a sexual deviant.

"One day, God will forgive you for what you did," I remembered Mrs. Pratt saying with sheer sincerity as I sat outside of the social worker's office before being transferred from Alabama to South Carolina.

I remained silent, never mumbling a word as I sat on a cold steel chair with a black trash bag full of clothes.

"The facility we are sending him to is considered to be one of the best in the nation to help him with these types of behaviors," the young white woman began. "Mrs. Pratt, one of the most important things to help T'Shobi with this is support from both you and Reverend Pratt."

"No!" Reverend Pratt yelled, causing both Mrs. Pratt and the social worker to jump in fear. "This devil child will not receive any support from me or my wife. I hope he rots in hell!" He stared at me long and hard, as if he were about to attack me. I remembered feeling fear, yet numbness. At thirteen I had already become accustomed to pain and fear from the years of abuse and heartache I had already experienced.

As they both walked out of the Department of Social Services office, Mrs. Pratt looked back at me with tears in her eyes. I don't know if she was feeling guilt, or if she was truly sad to see me leave. When she finally got to the exit, she looked back and waved bye to me. I gave her my middle finger.

"Young man, that is not nice of you considering the fact that those people took you in when no one else wanted you, and you go and do the things that you did to that sweet woman," an older black woman said to me as she walked around the corner to inform my case worker that she would be one of the people to transport me to South Carolina.

The entire five-hour drive, I was forced to listen to gospel music and Bible verses from the two transporters, who were informing me that I still had a chance to be forgiven by God for all of my transgressions. They also informed me that forcing myself sexually on a pastor's wife was one of God's ultimate sins, and that I needed to pray every night and every day to ensure He forgave me.

For nine months, I had to endure being chastised by the staff that worked there, as well as fight off several of the other boys that wanted me to be their lover. I was the youngest and smallest resident on the unit. Every day was an experience, but the one night I will never forget is the night another resident came into my room when the third shift staff had fallen asleep.

I was lying in my bed when suddenly, I was shaken awake. When I looked up, I saw a penis in my face; then I heard someone speak to me.

"Suck this, and you better not say a damn word, or I will kill you."

This went on for most of my stay at the facility. I became the resident dick sucker and everybody's toy. I was originally told that I would have to be there until I turned eighteen, but after my therapist there discovered that I was actually a victim and not an offender, they were able to have me released and I was placed back in foster care

Around two A.M. on that Friday after Justine's accident, I decided to check my messages from the entire week. Most of them were from Tinisha or Seth, but the only one that stood out, and the only person who had called that I had a desire to talk to, was my MeeMa.

"Baby, the Lord had you on my mind. Call me when you get this message."

After hearing her message, suddenly I began to feel completely sober. I could even smell the stench that was created from not showering for days. I emerged from the floor and walked to the bathroom. When I looked in the mirror, I was almost afraid of who I saw staring at me. It wasn't me. It wasn't the man I had become after all of the adversity. I saw the man that could have been me if I wasn't the strong person that, even after the pain, somehow still emerged from the sewage of disaster.

After taking a long, hot shower, I climbed into my bed for some much-needed sleep, hoping that I could have a peaceful night with no bad dreams.

I woke up to a loud banging on my door. I quickly threw on some sweats and a T-shirt and ran toward the door. Tinisha was standing there with a strange stare on her face, wearing a black trench coat and red high-heeled shoes.

"Take me," she said as she opened the trench coat, exposing her almost naked body.

21

Tinisha

T'Shobi quickly pulled me into his apartment after I showed him my offering. After my long prayer with God earlier that morning, I was willing and more than ready to experience my first real moment with a man. I wanted him to be the one to give me what I desired the most. I wanted him to make me feel like I had never felt before.

"Tinisha, what the hell is wrong with you?" he asked after closing his door.

"Baby, you are what's wrong with me. I want you to fuck me," I said, not believing my choice of words.

He walked over toward his couch then sat down. As I looked closely on the floor, I noticed bottles of beer and liquor, and what looked like a joint. I was shocked to see all of that. I never thought that he used drugs or that he drank, but at that moment, I really didn't care. I just wanted him to take me

"Are you going to fuck me?" I asked.

"Tinisha, you need to go home," he said without any expression.

That wasn't the answer I wanted to hear. I wanted him to enjoy what he saw then tell me yes, he was going to give it to me good and make me his wife.

I let my trench coat drop to the ground, fully exposing my

body. I was only wearing my newly purchased red Victoria's Secret bra and thongs, and a red pair of Jimmy Choos.

"Seriously, Tinisha, you need to go home. I am not who or what you need in your life."

I remained standing for what felt like forever. Although I wanted to stay and convince him that he was what I wanted, I had to face the fact that maybe I really wasn't. I picked my coat up from the floor, put it back on, and then reluctantly walked out the door. I wanted to look back, but I knew if I had, he would have seen my tears.

I sat crying in the parking lot of his apartment building for twenty minutes. Before driving away, I looked up toward his apartment and saw him staring at me out of the window.

When I arrived home, knowing that my roommate was at work, I opened the door and immediately pulled off the coat. As I was heading toward my bedroom, my roommate's boyfriend suddenly opened the door to her room.

"Wow," he said, staring at my exposed body.

I quickly ran to my room, locked the door, and lay across my bed and cried myself to sleep.

22

Justine

"She's been in and out of consciousness for two days now," I heard my mother say.

"Have you talked with the doctor?" came from a voice that I hadn't heard in years. It was my sister.

"Not today, but yesterday he said that she was doing well and that she was definitely a fighter," my mother responded.

"Have you talked to Seth?"

"Seth can go to hell for all I care," my mother said with anger.

"Mama, you shouldn't say that."

"You should be saying the same thing. Don't act like you don't understand my disdain for him. I hate him almost as much as I hated y'all's damn daddy. May he *not* rest in peace."

There was a long silence, and then my mother began singing a hymn. I wanted to open my eyes to see and talk to my mother, but I couldn't. I knew, because I had seen T'Shobi earlier, that they could open, but for some reason, at that moment, they refused to do as I willed. I felt trapped inside of my body, unable to do anything.

"How was your drive from Tampa?" I heard my mother ask.

"We arrived last night."

"Jonathan is with you? Why didn't you bring him he—"

More silence; then I drifted back to sleep.

***

I wasn't sure how long I had been asleep, but when I began to hear people around me talk again, there were more voices in the room than before.

"Grandma, can I get you something?"

"Thank you, Frederick, but I am fine," my mother said to my son.

"You've been here since Monday, Grandma. Why don't you go to my house and get some rest?" my youngest son, Chase, said.

"Baby, your grandma is just fine. I am going to stay here and wait for my daughter to open her eyes. I want to be the first person she sees."

"Aunt Janice, I haven't seen you in forever," Chase said to my sister.

"I'm well. I hate that we're having a reunion because of this situation, but it is really good to see both of my nephews."

I heard more idle conversations, until I drifted back into my slumber.

23

Seth

"I accepted a job today," Brandi said over the phone.

"Where is the job? There in Columbia?"

"No, in Charlotte," she said calmly. "I start next week."

I didn't like the sound of that. For years she had told me that she wanted to move to Charlotte. When we were still serious, I was able to convince her that she was better off in Columbia. The first time she told me she was moving, I actually offered to pay the lease on her condo. The second time, I bought her a Porsche.

"I don't think it's a wise idea, Brandi," I said as I was trying to come up with something to offer her to remain in Columbia.

"Seth, my mind is made up this time. I was offered a great salary, and the position places me in upper management."

"Why are you doing this to me?" I asked.

"This has nothing to do with you. You've known for years that I wanted to leave Columbia, and I'm sure you knew that eventually it was going to happen."

"Things would be much easier if you stayed there, or at least moved to another city."

"Seth," she began, "if I was going to reveal us, don't you think I would have by now? This has nothing to do with you or with us. I was offered a great position with great pay. Why should I turn down a wonderful opportunity because my *secret* part-time lover tells me to?"

As much as I wanted to argue my point to her, I realized that her mind was already made up and no matter what I said or offered, she was still coming to invade the city I called home.

We both sat in silence. I was still hoping to find a way to keep her in Columbia. I wanted this part of my life to be as far away from my *real* world. I knew without a doubt that by combining the two in the same city, nothing but chaos would come out of it.

"Do you need a new place? What about a new car?"

"Seth I am moving to Charlotte. Case is closed. I will be staying at the Comfort Inn Suites until I find a place to stay. I will be back tomorrow afternoon. If you want to see me, you know the room number."

"So, there's nothing I can do or say?" I asked, still praying that she would reason with me.

"My mind is completely made up. By the way, how is your wife?"

She caught me off guard with that question.

"Hunh?"

"I went to visit her on Monday. It was kind of interesting, too, that I ran into your musician as I was leaving." There was a long pause. "By the way, how were you able to get him as the musician at your church? I know you're on TV and all, and got a little sumtin-sumtin going, but a Grammy award winner playing every Sunday for you . . . you must have more swag than I thought you had," she said, giggling before hanging up the phone.

***

When I walked into my wife's hospital room, both of my sons were sitting on opposite sides of her, while her mother lay asleep on the couch.

"What's going on, Pops?" Frederick said after noticing me.

I gave both of my sons hugs then walked over and kissed Justine on the forehead.

Watching Justine lay quiet and bruised, I saw something in her that I had never seen before: peace. It seemed that for years after we married, peace was something I never saw or felt from her, almost as if she thrived on confusion.

"Hmph! So, you did remember that you had a wife lying near death in the hospital," her mother said as she arose to a sitting position on the couch.

"Good to see you also, Mabel," I said, giving her a fake smile.

"I've been here since Monday afternoon, and this is the first time I've seen you, Seth."

"You must have forgotten that I am the head of very large organization, and even during my own personal tragedies, I have business to attend to," I said as I looked away from her and back toward my wife.

"Did you just say an organization?" she asked with anger.

Both of my sons got up from their chairs and quietly walked out of the room. The back and forth with their grandmother and me was nothing new to them. It was something that had been going on for more than thirty years, and the only way I ever thought it would end would be as a result of one of us dying.

"Seth, you are supposed to be the pastor of a church that's leading folk to Christ, not the CEO of a multi-million dollar corporation," she said, adjusting her blouse that had become slightly twisted from her nap on the couch.

"Excuse me, Mabel. I am the pastor of a church, leading His flock to Christ, but I also realize that in order for the flock to flourish, you also have to be business-minded as well. We are no longer in the time of *We Shall Overcome*. Newsflash, some of us actually overcame."

"Boy, don't you dare sass me!" She quickly emerged from her chair. "I've known you since before you basically knew yourself. I remember when your daddy wouldn't dare allow you to talk to me or any elder with no respect."

She stormed toward the entrance of the room. Once she held the door latch, she looked back. "I never in my life thought that I could hate. God tells us that we must love everyone, and for years I asked God to please not allow you to be that technicality that hindered me from walking those Golden Streets. Seth Carlton Reynolds, I hate you, and I hate you even more for the pain you caused my family," she said before walking out, slamming the door behind her.

My heart felt as if it had dropped, and for a brief moment, I was beginning to feel hate also. I felt it burning in my soul. I turned my focus to Justine, and when I did, our eyes met. For several cold minutes, we stared at one another; then she closed her eyes.

24

T'Shobi

"I went to see Sister Pratt last Sunday," MeeMa said about an hour into our conversation.

I suddenly became silent. The conversation was going well until she brought up the name of the lady I strongly believed help to create my fucked up life.

"So, how is your garden this year, MeeMa? Get a lot of tomatoes?"

"Baby," she began, "I know that there are things in our lives that are hard to deal with and talk about, but there comes a time when we just have to. Sometimes talking about it helps us to heal."

"What about Roscoe? How is he? He should be what, eighteen now? Has he applied to any colleges? You know I will take care of it," I said, referring to my foster brother.

"Roscoe is doing fine, baby. He's doing just fine," she said, finally giving up on me talking about Mrs. Pratt.

After hanging up with MeeMa, I was actually feeling a lot better. With the exception of the brief mention of the beast that helped to create the pain in my life, we actually had a great conversation. I promised her that I would be in Alabama real soon to see her, and that I would do a whole lot better with staying in contact.

I spent the remainder of the day basically chilling out and regrouping. It had been a long time since I had an episode like that one. The only difference was that the last time I got into a funk, I packed my clothes into a car and left. As much as I tried to deny it to myself, my childhood made me a confused man.

After I fixed a quick lunch, I decided to ride out for a few. I had been in the Charlotte area for nearly seven months before I remembered that the facility I was placed in fourteen years ago was less than twenty minutes away from my apartment.

Driving down I-77 from Charlotte toward Rock Hill, South Carolina, I thought about turning around several times, but MeeMa's words from earlier continued to flow through my mind, allowing a small step of healing to take place.

There was a bank located next to the old building that I once called home. I couldn't remember if the bank had been there then. As a matter of fact, there were a lot of buildings nearby that housed small businesses that appeared new.

I drove my car into the parking lot of the bank and sat there for moments, staring at the recreation field located directly in front of the facility. When I noticed a group of kids walking out onto the field in a straight line, memories of my stay there hit me all at once, causing a stream of tears to flow down my face uncontrollably.

"Remember," I whispered to myself. "This is part of the healing."

***

I arrived back home around six that evening, and from a distance, I noticed Tinisha's car parked in front of my apartment. I decided not to drive toward my building, and drove around instead. I noticed she had perched herself in front of my door, waving her hands around, and I assumed she was praying.

Stalkers were not new to me, but she had definitely taken things to a new level. She was not someone I needed to deal with at the moment, so I decided to go and get something to eat. As much as it hurt, due to what had happened almost a week earlier, I chose to go back to Addie's.

Sitting at my table alone, eating fried plantains, I noticed a stunning woman walk into the restaurant. Her complexion was as smooth as a chocolate bar, and she wore long locks that she allowed to flow freely.

She was beautiful. She was lovely. She was . . . in my face.

"Hello," she said as she walked by, headed toward the counter.

I had my glass of tea tilted, ready to take a sip. My eyes remained on her, never blinking, hoping to capture every ounce of her being. I was so mesmerized with her that I missed my mouth, allowing tea to flow freely onto my pants.

"Aw, did the baby drop his tea?" she said as she walked past me again, taking her to-go bag with her out the door.

"Dat woman be so fine, she make he miss he whole mouf," an older Jamaican man said, laughing as I walked toward the bathroom to clean myself.

Although I was wet and miserable from my accident, I still drove home slowly, hoping that Tinisha would be gone by the time I got there. But just as luck would have it, she was still there; this time, with company.

"Officers, what seems to be the problem?" I asked the two cops standing behind Tinisha, who was kneeling at my door.

25

Tinisha

When I woke up from crying on my pillow, I prayed to God again for direction, and as always, He told me to continue in the pursuit for my man. I got up from the bed and went back to his apartment, but this time, unlike earlier, I was fully clothed.

When I walked out of my room, I heard the TV on in the front room. I walked around the corner and saw my roommate's boyfriend sitting on the couch, holding a beer with one hand, and the other inside his sweats. I wasn't quite sure, and I was too afraid to really look his way, but it appeared as if the hand he had in his pants was moving up and down.

"What up, sexy?" he said, causing a fear inside of me that made me practically run out the door.

Before leaving to go to T'Shobi's, I sat in my car and called my roommate to inform her that I was in no way comfortable with her boyfriend being there when she was not home. She didn't seem to be happy with what I said, but I really didn't care.

I drove to T'Shobi's house slowly, so that I could have a long talk with God to ask for guidance on what to do next.

When I got there, I noticed his car wasn't in the parking lot, so I did what God told me to do: pray until he arrived home. I'm not sure how long I was there, but I knew it was for a length of time. As his neighbors would pass by going to their apartments, I could hear them make comments.

"That chick is crazy."

"Is she still here?"

"He must have whipped it on her hard. Shorty kinda fine though. She oughta come and pray at my door. I definitely got some blessings for her."

I ignored them all and continued praying until . . .

"Excuse me, ma'am," a strong male voice said. "Ma'am, can you please get up?"

I remained on my knees in prayer, asking God to hear my cry and send T'Shobi home.

"Officer, she been there for at least three hours. But this is not the first time. All week she's been coming over here. I don't think the guy that lives here wants her around," I heard one of T'Shobi's female neighbors say.

"Ma'am, I'm going to have to ask you to leave the premises now or you will be arrested," the officer began again.

I remained on my knees, still praying, when I finally heard T'Shobi's voice.

"Officers, what seems to be the problem?"

"Sir, do you know this woman?" the officer asked. "We've received several complaints about her perched here at your door."

"Yes, officer, I do know her, and I will take care of the situation."

When the officers left, I opened my eyes and noticed the look of aggravation on T'Shobi's face.

"Come in," he said after opening the door.

I slowly got up from the ground and walked into the apartment, shutting the door behind me.

"Tinisha, this has to stop."

"But, T'Shobi, baby, God—" I started before being cut off.

"Tinisha, this has to stop *now!*"

"But Sunday at dinner . . ." I tried again.

"The next time you show up here, I will have the cops carry you to jail," he said then walked to the door, opening it, giving me my cue to leave.

I drove around town for hours, confused. From the first day I heard T'Shobi's voice on the radio when I was seventeen, God told me that he would be my future husband. I had followed his career from the beginning. When most of my girls in high school were drooling over Usher and Cisco from Dru Hill, my love went to a gospel artist named T'Shobi Wells.

Driving all around Charlotte with no set destination, I thought about the first day I saw him in person, when he came to New Deliverance. I felt as if I had died and gone to heaven. I knew without a doubt, because of God's revelation many years earlier, that if he was there, God was telling me he was mine. It was hard to believe that the man I had loved from afar for so many years was sitting only a few feet away from me.

After church that first Sunday, I rushed to meet him, and from that point on, I was on a mission that God had already told me was completed.

When I arrived home later that evening, all the lights were off. I heard soft music coming from my roommate's bedroom. As I got closer, I heard faint sensual moans.

"Yes," she whispered.

"Unnnnn," the male voice followed.

I quickly became aroused before the jealousy took over. I was supposed to be the one making the "yes" sound at that very moment, but instead, I was kicked out of his place and sent back to listen to the miserable voices of another couple.

After spending several moments listening, I went to my room, closing and locking the door behind me. I removed all of my clothes then lay on my bed.

The noises became louder and hard to block. Before I knew anything, my right hand started gently rubbing my clit.

"Shhhhh . . . yes . . . ooooooweeee . . . yes," I moaned.

Touching myself was definitely not new to me, but for some reason at that moment, listening to the sounds coming from the other room, with T'Shobi still heavy on my mind, I felt as if I were going into an orgasmic coma.

"Right there, baby. Right . . . there . . . awww . . . shit . . . fuuuck . . . meeeee. . . ."

After my third orgasm, I lay across my soaked sheets and fell asleep in my own essence.

26

Seth

"Is she coherent?"

"It's hard to say at this time, Mr. Reynolds," the doctor responded. "Although, the past couple of days, she's opened her eyes a couple of times."

After witnessing the opening of her eyes, I contacted the nursing staff to inform them that she may have awakened. I know it may have been a terrible thing, but when our eyes met and we stared at each other, I became disappointed. Somewhere deep inside of me, a part of me didn't want her to make it through this.

"Does this mean she will have a full recovery?" I asked.

"Mr. Reynolds, your wife has a long road to travel. She's not out of the woods yet," he said. He wrote something on the chart by her bed and walked out.

I remained by her side twenty more minutes, watching her sleep or whatever it was she was doing at the moment. I knew her mother would be back soon, and I didn't care to be there when she returned, so I decided to leave.

When I reached for the latch to open the door, it suddenly opened.

"Hello, Seth," Justine's sister said.

"Janice, how are you? You're looking good," I lied.

It had been many years since I last saw her, and although she looked better than she did the last time we were in each other's company, she didn't come close to the beauty she once possessed. She was only a shell of the beautiful woman I used to love.

"You've always been a good liar," she said with a weak grin. "For a minute I almost believed you. Years have a way of making a person wise."

"How long have you been here?"

She walked by me and took a seat on the couch. As she attempted to make herself comfortable, she looked back toward me.

"I assume you are leaving. I'm sure that the great Seth Reynolds has more pressing matters to attend to than to stay with his ailing wife and have a meaningless conversation with her fallen baby sister."

"What are you talking about, Janice?" I asked.

"Seth, please just leave and go wherever, or to whomever, you were going."

"What makes you think I'm leaving?" I asked.

"Seth, I am not ten anymore. You can't make me believe your dick is a Hershey bar. Your lies played out with me many years ago."

"Janice," I began, but had no other words to follow.

"Seth, please just go. I don't want to hear anything you have to say," she said with her hand in the air.

"How is Jonathan?" I asked, not really sure why, then hating that I did ask.

Janice jumped up from the couch and swiftly walked in front of me.

"You got some fucking balls, don't you? You really better leave now before you find yourself in the room next door."

I had never seen that side of her. I guess the years she spoke of not only made her wise, but made her angry. And even if I did try to deny it, I knew that in many ways, her life, what it had become, was a result of my actions.

"I will continue to serve as your minister of music, if you like; however, I need to sever all other ties," T'Shobi said via voicemail.

I listened to the message nearly forty times before attempting to call him.

"T'Shobi, please answer your phone next time I call, or please just call me back," I pleaded.

After leaving the hospital, I drove to the church, hoping that somehow he just happened to be there. I even rode by his studio, but he wasn't there either. I didn't know where he stayed. He told me he preferred that we didn't have any of our rendezvous there, and that there was no reason I needed to know where he lived.

Around midnight, I finally gave up on talking to or even seeing him. I still couldn't pinpoint exactly how I got so hooked on him, but not communicating with him was driving me crazy.

I reached into my desk drawer and grabbed the bottle of liquor, poured the glass full, and guzzled it. I needed to get my mind away from everything; not only the thoughts of T'Shobi, but also the lingering thoughts of what I had done to Janice nearly thirty-seven years earlier.

I was lost in my thoughts for hours, until I was interrupted by the ringing of my phone.

"I'm waiting," Brandi said.

"Give me an hour," I responded and then hit the END button.

27

Justine

When I opened my eyes and saw Seth standing there, I wanted to jump off the bed and kick the shit out of him. Although he didn't have anything to do with why I was lying near death in the hospital, I still blamed him for ruining my life.

We stared at each other for a few moments before I closed my eyes again. As I lay there in silence, hoping that he would not stay long, I heard my room door open.

"Hello, Seth," I heard my sister say.

It had been almost fifteen years since I last saw her. After she gave birth to her son, Jonathan, she started using drugs, leaving me or my mom to care for him. For five years, Janice was in and out of rehab, unable to kick that demon. I just couldn't understand her. Although I had actually caught her and Seth in the act, her being an addict pained me more.

In that five-year period, her life and her look changed dramatically. Her hair was no longer naturally wavy, but kinky and matted. Her beautiful, flawless honey-brown skin had black spots throughout.

As I lay there listening to them talk, I wanted to open my eyes to see my baby sister, but hearing her voice brought back so much anger. I listened to every word spoken, wishing that God could miraculously heal me and I would emerge from my bed and kick the shit out of both of them.

As I continued listening, I heard something that damn near gave me a heart attack.

"Seth, I am not ten anymore. You can't make me believe your dick is a Hershey bar. Your lies played out with me many years ago."

My ears had to have been deceiving me. I knew what I heard, and although for years I never put anything past Seth, Janice's statement shocked the hell out of me.

After a few moments of anger-filled conversation, I heard Janice threaten that if he didn't leave, he would have his own room. When I heard the door close, my eyes were finally able to open, and I saw my sister.

She was not the beautiful woman she was twenty years ago, but she looked well; a lot better than the last time we had seen each other.

"Justine?" she asked through a stream of tears. "Are you awake?"

I tried moving my mouth to say something, but there was no sound to accompany my moving lips.

"Shhhh, don't try to talk," she said as she came closer to me. "You are going to be okay."

As we stared at one another in silence, our eyes did the talking. She realized I heard the conversation between her and Seth. She knew that I understood that her relationship with my husband didn't begin the day I caught them, but many years earlier.

28

T'Shobi

"I am seriously thinking I'm going to have to have her arrested," I said to Al as we sat at the sound booth, mixing a track we had just completed.

I was never good at making friends. It seemed that all my life, everyone I came in contact with wanted something from me. It was a good feeling to have someone to talk to about things and feel comfortable knowing that he didn't want anything from me.

"You know, I kind of miss having stalkers," he replied, laughing. "But I know what you're saying; it can get scary." He paused to take a sip of his water. "So, are you dating anyone? And if not, why?"

I stared down at the controls on the board and began moving them nervously. I wanted to explain my life to him, but my guard wanted to rise.

"I have personal demons," I said.

"Bruh, who doesn't?"

My mind told me I could talk to him; that he would understand and maybe share some insight on how I could live in peace.

"I was molested at the age of ten," I started.

***

My instincts were right. Al was someone I could trust; someone who could pray for me and be a mentor, a big brother I never had, a friend that didn't require anything from that friendship.

For hours, we sat in the studio and I shared my entire life story with him. I even told him about Seth and Justine.

After talking about it, I began to feel better, as if a load had been removed from me. I finally understood what MeeMa meant by the healing process.

When I arrived home that evening, I was relieved that I would actually be able to walk up my stairs and not see Tinisha. All week she had basically invaded my personal space, something that I took great pride in protecting.

In every city I had lived, with the exception of Atlanta, I always stayed in apartments. I was never one to stay in one place too long, so I never saw the need to purchase a real home. After receiving my first major deal when I was twenty-one, I bought MeeMa a house and made sure she was taken care of.

As soon as I walked into my apartment, my phone rang. I had been avoiding the call all week. I knew this would come after I left the message the day before, ending all other dealings other than church-related with Seth. Somewhere in my thoughts, I knew that the call would create an urge for him to become even more aggressive in contacting me. I wondered if that's why I did it, still needing the assurance of someone wanting me, even if it was for his own selfish gain.

"Hello, Seth," I said, finally deciding to talk to him.

"Why have you been avoiding me?"

There were so many answers to that question, yet none that I felt he would understand. I knew how men like Seth were. They loved the thrill of something different in their lives. It was a fantasy, and if they were lucky enough to fulfill it, they came to crave it, and in some cases, they became obsessed.

"Seth, I have a lot going on, and honestly, I really need the time alone," I said.

"Where's your girlfriend?"

"Seth, this has nothing to do with her, or even with you, for that matter. This is about me."

"Can we see each other tonight?"

"No. I will see you at church tomorrow morning, Pastor Reynolds," I said then hit the END button on my phone, holding it long enough to shut it off.

I knew that my days of playing for New Deliverance were very close to being over. There was no way I would be able to continue as the minister of music there. And once again, Atlanta crossed my mind.

Bishop Randall Cole and I met three years earlier at The Stellar Awards. Backstage after my performance, he walked over to introduce himself to me. I knew who he was already. He was one of the very first pastors to gain that superstar status for ministry.

"You are a gifted artist," he said, licking his lips. "What else are you good at?"

I stared at the tall, dark, and burly man, finding him to be almost gross, with his thick mustache and clean-shaven bald head. He had to have been nearly three hundred pounds, but he carried himself as if he were the most attractive person in the world.

"Thanks. I appreciate that, and to answer your question, my talents are of a vast measure," I said, letting him know I understood his question.

That night, I was in his hotel room servicing him; that next morning, he invited me to come to Atlanta and serve as his minister of music, amongst other things. For months, his wife, Maria, made several passes at me, and although I knew it was risky, I finally accepted her invitation.

I had become extremely comfortable in Atlanta, maybe a little too comfortable, even choosing to purchase a house. For once in my life, I had become reckless. Years of frustrations can sometimes make you live a life of not caring about yourself or others.

Maria and I were meeting at our normal hideaway. She was on her knees, and I was positioned behind her, inducing pain that she found to also be pleasure. She was screaming, telling me how much it hurt, how much it felt so good. She told me to stop, then to thrust even harder.

As I was about to reach my point, I heard the door open. I looked back, and there was Randall. I quickly pulled my member out of her, causing her to become upset.

"What the hell you do that for, T'Shobi? I was just about to cu—" She stopped after turning around to see her husband staring at us.

"Randall, wha . . . what are you doing here?"

He stared in silence. I was waiting for a fight. I had been with him the night before, but the scene was much different. It was me on my knees, and him telling me how good my ass felt to him.

As he continued to stare at me, Maria attempted to say something else. He raised his hand to her, instructing her to remain silent. His eyes never left mine, and mine never left his. He had me by many pounds, but I was ready to go to battle with him. I began to ball my fists when suddenly, he grinned.

"Randall, are you joining, or are you just going to stare at us? I was just about to cum real good," she said, confusing the hell out of me.

He unbuckled his pants and let them drop to the floor. "Go ahead," he said. "Finish what you were doing."

Even more confused, I turned to Maria, noticing her getting back into position.

"Come on, T'Shobi. Finish me," she demanded.

I returned to her, and shortly after placing my member inside of her, Randall went to the other side of the bed and allowed her to suck him. Once he became hard, Randall then looked at me, giving me the sign that he was ready to do me.

He moved behind me and entered me with vicious thrusts; the same ones I in return gave to Maria. It was exciting, yet at the same time revolting.

As I began to put my clothes on, they made love to each other passionately, as if I weren't there. I watched them for a few moments, feeling jealous for their connection. I knew it was a feeling that I could not have with either one. Driving home, I cried, wishing that love, or even just anything that felt like a real love, could come my way.

I knew that staying there was no longer an option for me. Although that moment with both of them felt pleasurable to me, I knew that eventually the situation would become a complicated triangle, so I did what I knew how to do best: I left.

The next day, I was in my car and headed to Charlotte, leaving all of my other belongings behind me.

It seemed as if my entire life was a battle. I dealt with the rejection of my mother. I had to cope with being molested and labeled a deviant due to the actions of my adoptive mother. I survived being raped by older boys.

I hated thinking about my past, because it left me empty,

frustrated, and alone. I didn't understand my emotions at times. I didn't understand how being with men felt right. I couldn't comprehend why I chose to deal with older women just to abuse them as I had been abused. My life was a constant struggle, and instead of trying things in a new way, I found myself migrating to the same situation with different people.

After falling asleep on the couch, reminiscing about the past, I turned my phone back on, and to my surprise, there were no new messages. I turned the TV on and began flipping channels, not really paying much attention to what was on when my phone rang.

The screen read UNAVAILABLE, and usually I avoided those calls, but something guided me to answer.

"Hello, Mr. Wells," the sexy yet raspy voice said.

"Who am I speaking with?"

"You had an accident yesterday regarding some tea, correct?"

I was baffled. I wondered if it could really be her; and if it was, how did she get my phone number?

"Yes," I said slowly.

"Well, I would like to apologize and offer any assistance to you for the embarrassment that may have cost you."

"How did you get my number?" I asked.

"Mr. Wells, let's just say I am a woman that, when I want something, I have my ways of getting it." She giggled. "Where can we meet?"

29

Tinisha

I spent all day that Saturday lying on my bed, repeating what I had done all night: masturbate.

Although I was alone, I could feel T'Shobi's presence. He was there with me, stroking me, kissing me, making me cum over and over and over again. I was in pure bliss.

Late that evening, I heard my roommate and her boyfriend arguing.

"Why are you listening to her?" I heard her yell.

"What you talking about, Trice? Ain't nobody listenin' to nobody."

"Damn it, Malik, you pissing me off," she said.

"Trice, you know damn well I ain't thinking about that chick. She too holy," he said.

"Then why you stop at the door when you walked by her room?"

"'Cause that shit funny." He began laughing. "For a minute I thought she had a nigga up in there tapping it."

After hearing him say that, I turned over on my stomach and began crying. I was in misery, wanting to be loved, wanting to feel special, and an insignificant gnat was laughing at me, causing tears to continually fall from my eyes.

I was sheltered basically all of my life. My mother refused to allow me to do anything or even have friends.

"As long as you got the Lord, baby, you will be just fine," she used to tell me as a little girl when I would have to turn down invites to slumber parties.

I was an excellent student and had many scholarships to schools across the country, but because of my mother's over protectiveness, I remained home in Greensboro and attended Bennett College, an all girls school. I majored in history with hopes of going to law school, but again, my mother was against that.

"Don't you know lawyers are the devil's workers?"

After college, I remained home for two years, the length of time it took for me to convince her that I was ready to tackle the world on my own. She was reluctant to let me go, and if it had not been for my father's help, I would probably have been living under their roof.

"Malik!" I heard Trice yell right outside of my door. "Why are you standing at Tinisha's door with your head stuck to it?"

"What you talking about? I was just walking by, going to your room," he said.

"Malik, my room is on the other side of the hall, fool."

There was a long silence, but I could tell both of them were still standing there.

"You know what?" Trice began again. "I need to take a drive. Be gone by the time I get back," she said. I heard her grab her keys then walk out the door.

I got up from the bed then walked over to the window, watching her drive away in her car. When she was out of sight, I walked to the door, naked, and opened it.

When Malik came out of Trice's room, he stopped and looked over my body. I stared long and hard at him. He wore his hair in cornrows and had earrings in both ears. He had on a team jersey, and his jeans looked as if they were going to fall down any minute. He looked like a thug; a guy that if I brought him home, it would kill my mother.

"Damn, ma, your body bangin' too damn hard to be up in there doing yourself. Need some help with that?"

I walked over to him, kissed him softly on his mouth, turned around, and walked back to my room, leaving the door open.

30

Seth

I was so distraught that Sunday morning that I had to get one of my associates to preach, while I remained in my office, watching the service from my flat screen TV. As I sat behind my desk, basically staring at the screen, for whatever reasons, the camera zoomed in on a dark and beautiful woman walking into the church. I stared at the screen then noticed who it was—Brandi.

The night before, I tried calling her, but she never answered the phone. I wondered where she could have been that she couldn't answer my calls. When I was with her on that Friday evening, she did something that I definitely didn't expect her to do.

"Where did you get the food from?" I asked her when I walked into her suite. She had carryout trays of jerk chicken, plantains, and red beans and rice.

"Addie's," she said nonchalantly.

"That's where Justine had her accident," I said softly.

We sat and ate in silence, creating a strange and eerie feeling for me.

"Why are you so quiet?" I asked.

"No reason. Just have some things on my mind."

"Why did you move here?" I asked.

Brandi stared at me for a few moments then arose from the chair and walked to the bedroom. She came back with a small black bag and handed it to me. When I opened it, I noticed two sets of keys.

"What is this?"

"These are the keys to the Porsche," she said, picking up each set one by one. "And these are the keys to the town-house in Columbia. When you get done eating, please go." She walked back to the room, closing and locking the door behind her.

"Why are you here?" I whispered to myself as I continued to watch the service.

After services were over, I called her cell phone to ask her to meet me in my office, but the call went directly to her voice-mail.

I called for my security team to come and get me so that I could walk through the congregation without being swamped by the thousands of members leaving.

When we made our way through the crowd, I saw a scene that damn near gave me a heart attack. Both of my lovers, standing side by side, laughing as if they had known each other for years.

31

Justine

Six Months Later

"Baby, can I get you anything?" my mother yelled from the kitchen.

"No, Mama. Thanks, but I'm fine," I yelled back as I was trying to adjust myself in the bed. "Has anyone heard from Seth?"

"No, child. Now, hush and relax. The doctor said for you to remain stress free, and that's exactly how we're going to have it," she said as she brought a tray full of food to me.

"Mama, I told you I didn't need anything," I said, already knowing that she didn't care what I said.

"You need to eat," she said, placing the tray in front of me.

I had been home from the hospital for less than a week, and my sorry-ass husband was still nowhere to be found. It had been over four months since anyone had seen him.

While in the hospital, a detective came to my room to ask questions.

"Mrs. Reynolds, do you know of anyone that had any grievances with your husband?"

"No," I lied.

Of course I knew, being the first in line myself, followed by my sister, and I'm sure a long list of others. But I couldn't tell the detective. If I told them about Janice's life story, they would have her listed as the prime suspect.

"What about at the church? Is there anyone that you know of that may have wanted to harm Pastor Reynolds?"

"Officer," I began, becoming irritated with this line of questioning, "I've been in this hospital for two months now. Do you honestly think that I could know anything?"

"Ma'am, I understand that this is an inconvenience for you, but we are looking at this as possibly being something planned for months, or even years, not just in recent days," he said before writing something on his pad before walking out the door.

Now, four months after the detective came to visit me, Seth was still missing. I was actually happy as hell that the bastard wasn't around. The only part that I felt bad about was the fact that if he was dead, whoever killed him left me out to get a piece of his sorry pedophile ass.

For years, I was mad at my sister. I had even hated her at one point. Not only had she slept with my husband, but she also bore his child. Then she became an addict. She had so much promise, so much talent, and at the time, I just saw her as an absolutely pathetic hussy.

That day at the hospital, after hearing the conversation between her and Seth, I could honestly say that if I were able to at that moment, I would have killed his ass. To be honest, although she never mentioned anything about him or their past, I secretly believe that she had something to do with his disappearance.

"Why are you not eating your food?" my mom said, returning to the bedroom to check on me.

"Mama, I told you I was fine."

"And I told you that you need to eat," she said as she sat down beside me and began feeding me like I was a baby.

32

Tinisha

"TiTi, I'm going to leave Trice," Malik said to me as he lay in the bed beside me.

"Why?"

"To be with you," he said, leaning over to kiss me.

I quickly pulled away from him and grabbed my clothes off the chair on the other side of the room.

"Baby, where you going?"

"I have somewhere to be in a couple of hours. Besides, Trice will be home soon," I lied.

"Fuck Trice. TiTi, baby, it's all about you," he said, walking up behind me and kissing the nape of my neck.

As the days went by, I was beginning to hate that I ever started sleeping with him. Whoever said that the first person you sleep with you will love for life told nothing but a lie. Malik was only a temporary solution to my problem at the time. It wasn't supposed to have lasted for six months, and he definitely wasn't supposed to fall in love.

"I'm serious, baby. I want us to be together," he said again as he gathered his clothes then walked to the other side of the hall to Trice's room.

I had to hurry up and do something about him. It wasn't what I desired, and my heart still belonged to T'Shobi, even if he did have a new woman.

After he threatened to have me sent to jail if I came back to his house, I decided to let things calm down for a while before I started to try again, but it was still my mission to make him mine. I still believed what God told me about T'Shobi being my husband.

After taking a long shower, I decided to take a ride to visit First Lady Reynolds. Since her accident, then the strange and sudden disappearance of Pastor Reynolds, my heart really went out to her.

I had to go into a seriously deep prayer after her accident, because I was really hoping that she would die, but that was only because I knew she and T'Shobi were having an affair. I needed her to step away.

Now I had new competition, Brandi Myles. Now it was her I had to get rid of.

"Tinisha, it's good to see you again," First Lady Reynolds said as I walked over to kiss her cheek.

"You are looking very well, First Lady," I said, noticing that she had very few visible scars on her face. "Are there any new developments on Pastor Reynolds?" I asked.

"Dear heart, I know you mean well, but we are not discussing that situation in this house. My daughter is under strict orders to remain stress free, and that's exactly what we're doing, remaining stress free," her mother said, walking in from another room.

"Excuse my mother, Tinisha. She's just being a mother," First Lady said with a smile.

I sat and talked with her for about twenty more minutes before deciding to leave. I had nowhere else to go, but I didn't want to stay around too much longer.

I was walking toward my car when I heard a male voice calling my name. When I looked back, I noticed their youngest son Chase walking toward me.

"How have you been? I don't get a chance to talk to you much since you left the choir," he said as he reached in to hug me.

Chase had Pastor Reynolds's height, but he had many of First Lady Reynolds's features, making him a very attractive man.

"I've been extremely busy at work, and I'm in the process of returning to school," I said.

"Okay, just wanted you to know that I miss seeing you at practice. You know T'Shobi is using the choir to sing background on his new album," he said.

"That is wonderful."

We stood staring at one another for a few moments in silence. I could tell he wanted to say something else to me, but wasn't sure if he should.

"Chase," I said softly, breaking our silence. "Do you want to fuck me?"

His eyes widened and his mouth dropped from my boldness.

"Uhh . . . err . . . uhh . . . I–" was all he could say before his wife called him from the front porch.

"I can make it happen if you want," I said, walking away to my car, leaving him there looking like a puppy contemplating which master to choose.

33

T'Shobi

I never thought it was possible, but I realized a lot of things could happen in six months. I was finally feeling as if I had a full-scaled life. Everything was working for the good. I was able to come to terms with a lot in my life, and it would have been a total error on my part if I had not given Brandi partial credit for it. But I had to admit I almost didn't allow her into my life at first.

Six months earlier, being the person that I am, I was totally cautious. Her calling me out of the blue honestly scared the shit out of me, regardless of how attractive I thought she was. All I could think of was that I had another Tinisha to deal with.

After much convincing that I could trust her during that first phone conversation, we decided to meet at The Jazz Café in south Charlotte. When I arrived there, I scanned the room looking for her to no avail. When the keyboardist from the band recognized me, he asked me to come and sit in and play a couple of songs with them. I was reluctant at first, but it had been so long since I played anything other than gospel that I decided to jump on the opportunity to jam.

After about thirty minutes of playing, I exited the stage, and to my surprise, Brandi was standing right in front of me.

"You're quite a talented brother on those keys, Mr. Wells," she said, showing me her perfect smile. "Let's grab a table."

"So, tell me. How did you get my number?"

"My, aren't we the curious one?" she said, still smiling.

"I've been a cautious person most of my life."

"I understand," she said, becoming serious. "In no way did I intend to make you nervous, T'Shobi, and I promise in time you will find that I am definitely someone you can trust."

"You are one of a thousand people to tell me that in my lifetime," I responded, still cautious of this woman I had seen only once.

We sat for an hour in the dimly lit room, and to my surprise, I did feel comfortable with her. We decided to leave and go to her place.

"Please overlook the mess. I actually just moved in today," she said as she opened the door to her condo.

"You seem to be doing well for yourself," I said, admiring her spacious domain.

"In spite of it all, I've been blessed."

As we walked over to the couch in her sitting area, I realized that for the first time since seeing her at the restaurant, she did look familiar to me.

"I've seen you somewhere before."

"Yes, you saw me yesterday at the restaurant," she said with a devilish grin.

"No, I've actually seen you somewhere before yesterday. I just can't put my finger on where."

"Maybe I just have one of those faces that make you think you've seen me," she said, taking off her heels and sitting down on the couch beside me.

We began talking more, and again I found myself feeling comfortable around her, something that was definitely out of character for me.

As we sat with the TV on, having conversation, she leaned forward and gave me a short yet sweet kiss on my lips. She did this several times before we actually went at a battle of tongues with one another. Her kisses turned me on, and I felt myself heat up. Just that quick, I found myself actually desiring a woman, and not despising her for what someone else had done to me years earlier.

I placed my hand under the brown retro T-shirt she wore and began to play with her small breasts. I lifted the shirt over her head and swiftly unhooked her bra, exposing them then sucking each one slowly.

"You making me hot," she said, barely whispering.

I continued sucking her breasts as my hand traced her perfectly shaped body. I unbuttoned her well-fitted jeans, while she invited the opportunity. My hand continued to move south, heading for her southern treat, ready to play in the rivers that flowed, then . . . I remembered where I had seen her before.

"Surprise," she said with a slight grin.

34

Seth

I was finally on the verge of losing my mind. It had been months since I had seen the light of day, and I was almost convinced that my days would end in the basement where I was locked away. I continued to play in my mind the events that happened to land me in there. It was still very vague.

After seeing T'Shobi and Brandi talking after church, I immediately had security walk me toward them, but just as I assumed she would do, after noticing me coming their way, she grabbed him by the hand and walked toward the door. I then had security take me back to my office, where I attempted several times to call both of their cell phones.

"T'Shobi, you need to call me immediately," I began on his voicemail. "There's something you need to know about the woman you're with."

For two months, I struggled with the thought of the two of them together. I tried calling them several times, and even attempted to talk to them at church, but for obvious reasons, I was never able to have the type of conversation I needed to have.

My life felt like a huge hurricane had come in and wiped everything away. I was no longer functioning with a sane mind. I was losing everything that was important in my life.

My relationships with everyone had dove and completely crashed. Both of my lovers were now lovers. My sons were angry with me because I stopped visiting their mother, and the administrative board at the church was beginning to question my effectiveness as their pastor.

One evening, arriving home after a three-hour meeting with the board, my intention was to go straight to my office and sit alone and drink until I passed out. That never happened. Honestly, I have no idea what actually took place. The only thing I remembered was stepping out of my car and walking toward the door of my home. When I awakened, I was locked in the basement that provided me with a small kitchen that was once fully stocked with food, a bathroom with a shower, and a small nineteen-inch TV.

I wasn't sure, but I couldn't help but think that Brandi was behind this. At one point, I was thinking this was an act of Janice, because every now and again I would wake up and notice newspaper articles left on the floor with highlighted headlines referring to child molestation.

I may have been wrong for what I did to her, but I didn't feel like I was totally to blame. Our families had basically forced Justine and me on each other. I knew my father was aware of my desires for younger girls, and although I didn't act on them until I met Janice, he knew my issues, and instead of finding me the proper help, he had pushed me into dating Justine.

"Trust me, son. You will grow out of that. It's only a stage you're going through. Your mind has forgotten to grow along with your body," had been his lame explanation to my serious problem.

For the past four months, my days were basically the same. Although I knew the time of day, it was because of having the TV, not being able to see the rising of the sun. My body clock was shot to hell. I slept a lot, which I guess was a good thing because it allowed time to move faster. I was certain that whoever was responsible for this had something hidden in the food that made me sleep. Every time I ate or drank something, I would fall asleep. At one point, I tried not to eat, but that made me miserable. But as time continued to pass and it seemed that I was never leaving, sleep became a welcome friend.

I didn't know what was going on or exactly who was doing it, but I began to accept the fact that God's wrath had finally caught up with me.

35

Justine

I sat in church in my normal place in the front row. Although Seth was no longer there and no one knew where he was, they continued to treat me as the first lady of the church.

During the service, my focus stayed on T'Shobi. He had come to visit me a few times over the past few months, but he never stayed very long.

"I feel responsible for this," he often told me.

I explained to him several times that it was my stupidity, along with my ridiculously jealous spirit, that created the situation.

I had time to evaluate everything that was going on in my life while in the hospital. I was a fifty-one-year-old lady basically sexing a child. Although I was already aware of what I was doing, as my mind began to catch up with my age, I began feeling the guilt and shame of what I had done.

I wasn't happy at home, so I searched for my own sense of happiness in the form of a man who was two years younger than my youngest son. Not only did I focus on T'Shobi, I preyed on him.

When services were over, several members of the congregation came to where I was sitting as I waited for my son Chase to get my wheelchair.

As I talked with everyone, my focus, as earlier, remained on T'Shobi. Thoughts of being with him sexually, even those times where it felt as if he were attacking me, were beginning to make me want him at that very moment. I kept my eyes on him as he was packing up his keyboard while talking to a beautiful, tall, and slim woman.

"That must be the love of his life everyone has been talking about," I whispered to Janice.

"Trust me, big sis, she's not what you think she is," she responded.

Janice's comment raised my curiosity, and although I wanted to know more, I left it alone. Since overhearing the conversation between her and Seth, I made it a point to start treating her as a sister and not as my enemy. She was the victim of a vicious act done by my boyfriend, who later became my husband.

"Is that the love of your life I've heard so much about?" I asked T'Shobi when he came to greet me before leaving.

We both looked in her direction at the same time.

"Yes, that's Brandi," he said with a wide smile on his face.

"I'm glad that you're happy," I said, half lying, half telling the truth.

I had already accepted the fact that anything between us ended the night I was struck by the car. It was time for me to be a woman that looked out for my family. The accident really wasn't an accident, but a lesson I definitely needed to learn.

After our brief conversation, I watched the two of them walk away. I don't know why, but an eerie feeling came over me, leading me to believe that there were more things I was about to learn.

"What is taking Chase so long to bring my wheelchair?" I asked Janice.

"He's over there talking to some girl," she said, pointing.

When I looked up, I saw Chase in what appeared to be a heated conversation with Tinisha.

"Can you tell him I am ready to go?" I said. For some reason, I was not feeling comfortable seeing my youngest son talk to her.

36

Tinisha

"Hello, T'Shobi," I said as I passed him and his *friend*.

I was far from being over him, but my alter ego, TiTi, couldn't give a damn about him.

TiTi was a godsend for me. She allowed me to do things that I would never have dared to do. I don't know exactly when she surfaced, but I remembered months ago, when I went off on my roommate and her boyfriend, I heard a voice speaking to me; then she appeared and allowed Malik to sex her.

When I passed them, I ran into Chase.

"Can I see you later?" he asked.

"I already have plans," I lied.

He was a sorry fuck, and honestly, I could have done better doing myself.

"Change them."

I giggled, not believing that he thought he was worth me dropping any and everything I had going on.

"Negro, please," I said, attempting to walk away.

"How are you going to treat me this way?" he said, grabbing me by the arm.

"First of all, you need to remove your hand," I said, staring him directly in his eyes. "Secondly, who in the hell do you think you are, you small-dick, non-pussy-eating bastard."

He stared at me in disbelief of TiTi's brutal honesty.

"You are a bitch."

"Thanks. I appreciate that," I said with a smile then walked away.

When I arrived back to my apartment, Malik was sitting on the couch, watching TV.

"Do you even have a place of you own?" I asked, walking to the refrigerator to get a bottle of water.

"You know I do," he said in a low voice. "You remember what happened the last time you were there, don't you?"

I rolled my eyes at him, and then, with no other words, walked to my room, closing and locking the door behind me. I sat on my bed for a few minutes, and suddenly, Tinisha began crying.

Although being TiTi was fun, she was living recklessly. All of my life, I was accustomed to a structure, but TiTi was all about doing whatever.

As I lay on the bed, my phone rang.

"Why the hell are you calling me?" I asked.

"I want to see you tonight."

"No," I responded.

"Why not?"

"Not in the mood," I responded.

"Well, call me if you change your mind, okay?"

I hung up the phone and turned it off. As I removed my clothes and stared in the mirror, I began to rethink the offer.

"TiTi could use a good fuck right now," I whispered. "And unlike his baby brother Chase, Frederick not only has a big dick that he knows how to use, he can also eat the hell out of some pussy."

37

Seth

"Hello," I yelled after waking up to noises coming from the behind the closed door at the top of the stairs. "Who's there? Who has me down here? I demand that you release me now!"

Whomever I heard remained silent; then suddenly, the door opened. I tried to stand up and run toward the door, but fell down in my attempt. As I wobbled around on the floor, trying to get up, a newspaper flew down; then the door closed before I could see who was there.

"Who's there?" I yelled again, still receiving no response.

When I walked over to the paper, I read the headline: LOCAL MINISTER STILL MISSING AFTER 6 MONTHS: FOUL PLAY SUSPECTED.

Whoever was holding me was letting me know that in the eyes of the world, I was dead.

After reading the headline from the paper, I sat on the couch that also served as my bed. I turned on the TV to keep me company, but I felt my mind turning in a thousand circles. I had to move around; sitting was not the answer for me at that moment. I walked over to the small kitchen and tried to find something sharp so that I could finally end my life at that very moment.

"God, please forgive me," I cried as I tried to slit my wrist with the sharpest thing I could find, which was a butter knife.

38

T'Shobi

"How close are you?" Brandi asked me over the phone.

"About thirty minutes. Why? What's up?"

"I have a surprise for you when you get here," she said glee-fully.

After hitting the END button on the phone, I began to think about my new life. It was one that I actually enjoyed waking up to every morning; one that allowed me to truly understand what it was like to love, as well as to be loved.

Brandi brought a lot of understanding to my shattered world, and I would always be grateful to her for bringing some form of happiness into my life. But even in that there was something still missing.

Shortly after we began dating, I found her to be someone I could trust and be open and honest with. We were both that way with each other, sharing everything, keeping nothing a secret.

She helped me to understand and tackle my personal demons. After much prayer and debate against the idea, I decided to do two things before I could actually move forward in life: visit the facility that I once called home, volunteering in any way I could, and visit Mrs. Pratt.

The first was the easiest. For the past several months, I

taught a music class once a week to any of the kids interested in learning how to play an instrument. It was the second task that I had issues with, and one that I still hadn't acted upon.

Being in a relationship with a woman like Brandi, although it felt normal to me, somewhere within, I knew it just wasn't right. We couldn't have kids, and in reality, unless we were around similar couples, our relationship was basically a lie. Regardless of how much of a woman she looked like in public; regardless of how many estrogen pills she took to appear more like a woman; when it all came down to it, we were still two men in a relationship.

Given the fact that the only comfortable relationship I'd ever had was with her, and knowing that Mrs. Pratt's actions had led to me being placed in a situation to be violated over and over again by other boys, I was still having issues.

Brandi made me happy, but at the same time, I still found it hard not to wonder what my life would have been like if all that had happened in my past had never taken place.

Before going to Brandi's house I had to stop by my place to grab some clothes. As I walked up the steps to my apartment, I saw a sight that I thought I would never see again.

"Tinisha?" I asked, but received no response from her.

"No, bitch, I'm not Tinisha. My name is TiTi," she said with a strange look in her eyes.

"Okay . . . TiTi, what can I do for you?" I asked suspiciously

"Trust me, baby, you can't do a damn thing for me," she said with curled lips. "I just wanted to come by and see if I could see what it is she saw in you." She began looking me over. "Nothing from what I could see," she said then walked away.

I couldn't help but become concerned for her. Although she was already strange before, since the last episode when she showed up and the police were called, she had begun to act weirder. I had noticed her talking to several different men, and even caught her and one of Seth's sons in a compromising situation as I walked into the choir room.

"By the way, how are things with you and your *girl?*" she yelled from the bottom of the stairs.

I responded by walking into my place without answering her question.

After taking a quick shower, I got dressed then packed an overnight bag. On my way out the door, I noticed a yellow manila envelope that had URGENT: READ NOW written boldly on the front.

When I opened the folder and saw its contents, my heart felt as if it were about to explode. I quickly walked back into my place then read the letter that accompanied the pictures.

Watch your back! I know about you and Seth and Justine.

There was no name attached to the letter. That bothered me. At first I assumed it was Tinisha, but that thought quickly disappeared when my phone rang.

"Hello," I said, answering the unknown number.

"Mr. Wells, if you want the contents of this package to remain a secret, you will do exactly as I say," the disguised voice said, then followed with detailed instructions.

39

Justine

I was worn out when I arrived home from rehab. I had literally worked my ass off to take three steps without a walker. My physical therapist was convinced that I would be able to walk again within a few months, and damn near guaranteed me that within the year I would be able to walk without the assistance of crutches or a cane. I couldn't help but realize how much I had taken for granted until I lost the most basic necessities of life.

"How are you feeling?" Janice asked me as she wheeled me to the car.

"I'm tired as hell and ready to go home and sleep."

Chase was at the house when we arrived, to help me get out of the car and into the bed. I had to give much credit to my boys. Throughout this entire ordeal, they had really been around to help out as much as possible.

As I lay in bed watching TV, my mother walked in with a tray of food, as always wanting me to eat something. "A detective called while you were in rehab," she said as she placed the food in front of me.

"Have they found his body?" I asked, wishing that the answer would be yes.

"No. He just stated that they really need to set up a time to talk with you."

After eating, I thought about calling the lead detective to inquire about his call, but instead, I hit the OFF button on the TV took a nap.

"Baby," my mother said, waking me up from my nap. "A detective is here," she whispered.

"Okay. Can you tell him to give me a few moments?"

"He's not here for you," she said, still whispering.

"Then why is he here? And why are you whispering?"

She walked into my room, closing the door gently. "He's talking to Janice."

"Why is he talking to her?" I said, trying to lift myself up.

"I don't know, but I don't like it."

I didn't like it either. I was afraid that somehow, the things that Seth did to her as a child had surfaced. I wasn't sure what the statute of limitations were, but I was more than certain that the crime he committed thirty years ago had far passed any type of punishment that he deserved.

"I don't like it either," I said as we both sat in silence, trying to hear as much of the conversation as possible.

A few moments later, we heard the front door close, and Janice walked into the room.

"Is everything okay?" I asked.

"If you are wondering if I had anything to do with Seth disappearing, the answer is no," she said with a slight attitude.

None of us ever accused her of being involved in Seth's disappearance, and to be honest, if she was involved, we would have understood.

"What did the detective want?" my mother asked.

"He wanted to know if I knew where Jonathan was," she said. Now concern was immediately rushing over her face.

For years, I had done the math; for years, although no one had to tell me, I knew. When I first realized it, I was bitter, even angry, and it pretty much, in my own opinion, gave me the right to do what I wanted to. But since Janice's return, I began to understand her situation more. I understood why she stayed away and never came to visit. I understood why we never got the chance to get to know her son.

"Why did he want to know where Jonathan was?" my mother asked.

Janice walked over to the window and began staring out of it. She remained silent for moments before speaking again.

"Because his father has been missing for six months," she said softly as she continued to look out the window.

40

Tinisha

"Hello," I spoke groggily into the phone.

"Praise God. Good morning."

"Go to hell," I said to my mother before hitting the end button to shut off the phone and go back to sleep.

I didn't feel like being bothered with her at 5:45 in the morning. It was just too damn early. It had been months since I did my morning prayer, and from the way it seemed, it would be more months, if ever, that I started back.

TiTi appeared to have finally taken over and was refusing to leave anytime soon. Every time I tried to send her away, she appeared more often and lived more recklessly.

I really knew she was out of control when she showed up at T'Shobi's apartment. As I listened to her talk to T'Shobi with so much aggression and boldness, I became scared. I was almost certain that he was going to call the police. I wanted to scream out to him and let him know that it was me that he was looking at, but TiTi was the one talking. She was the more dominant one. She had gained all control.

"TiTi, I'm feeling neglected over here," Malik said as I walked out of my room to leave for work. "It's been weeks since you let a brother get a taste. What's up with that?"

"I don't have time for you right now, Malik. I'm on my way to work."

"I miss you. You be gone all the time and I never see you around," he said as he grabbed me by my waist.

"Please remove your hands from my waist."

"Look here," he said as he moved his hands from my waist and placed them on my arms. "I know I was the first one to hit that. You supposed to love me forever."

I was beginning to wonder what the hell it was about men grabbing women by the arm forcefully. Did they really believe that it intimidated us? One thing is for sure, it may have scared Tinisha, but for TiTi, it gave her the power. Before he could say another word, my knee met his nuts and he dropped down to the ground.

"If you ever touch me again, I will kill you," I said as my knee met then his nose.

Later that evening when I arrived home, Trice was sitting on the couch holding a baseball bat.

"Malik told me you've been trying to come on to him. Is that true?" she said, holding the bat as if it would scare me.

"Trick—I mean Trice—please," I said with a smirk. "Don't nobody want that wannabe thug, country-ass Negro." I pointed to the bat. "And that is for . . . ?"

When she noticed the expression on my face was one that was ready for anything, she placed the bat down and began crying.

Tinisha wanted to console her, wanted to be there for her, but TiTi didn't give a damn, walking past her nonchalantly, heading to the bedroom.

"Bitch better check herself," I said loud enough for her to hear me. "Get fucked up in this piece."

41

Seth

When I woke up, I noticed a manila envelope sitting on the floor. It had the instructions LOOK NOW written on it. When I opened the envelope, I found several pictures of T'Shobi and me coming in and out of The Blake Hotel. I continued to look through the several pictures until I saw something that damn near took me over.

"Justine? T'Shobi? Together?"

I jumped up from the couch and walked toward the door that kept me locked in that dreadful basement.

"Brandi, I know that it's you behind this! I demand that you free me now!" I said, unsure if I was being heard.

After about twenty minutes of walking around and looking through the pictures over and over again, I sat back on the couch. I couldn't believe it. Justine and I were both having an affair with the same man.

42

T'Shobi

I called Brandi to let her know that our plans were going to have to change and that I would give her a call as soon as I could. Of course she was disappointed, but there was nothing I could really do about it at the moment. My life was about to become even more complicated if I didn't do as I was instructed.

After typing in the directions on the GPS, I began to wonder who could have been behind all of this, and who would have known about my affairs. Brandi knew, but she only knew after I told her. Or did she? I knew that Brandi and Seth had something at one time, and I even thought about him once warning me that she could be dangerous, but what would she have to gain by doing all of this?

My mind began rushing, and I didn't really know what to do, with the exception of what was told to me. The caller instructed that if I contacted anyone, my secrets would be exposed and my life as I knew it destroyed.

I couldn't help but think that if the person behind this really knew me, they would know that my life was destroyed a long time ago.

When I arrived at the location, a house on the south side of Charlotte, per my instructions, I got out of my car. I saw an envelope similar to the one left in front of my door. I was told to get the envelope, with definite instructions not to look in it, but to take it to Justine. It was already getting late, and I was exhausted and stressed, so I decided to wait until that next morning to take it to her.

I woke up early, still feeling nervous and apprehensive about all that had happened the night before. I checked my voicemail to see if I had any interesting calls that I might have missed.

"Baby," Brandi started, "it's eleven P.M. and I haven't heard from you since you stood me up," she said with a giggle. "Make sure you call me when you get this message."

"T'Shobi, this is TiTi. Call me on Tinisha's phone when you get this."

I began to wonder if Tinisha was behind all of this. I was almost certain she wasn't, but her new persona, TiTi, for all I knew, could have been capable of anything.

"T'Shobi," the disguised voice said, "time is wasting. I need for Justine to receive that package within the hour."

I looked over at the clock and noticed it was 9:30. I quickly jumped in the shower and then threw on some sweats and a long-sleeved tee, and ran to my car.

On the ride to Justine's, I continued to play different scenarios in my mind of who could have been behind all of this.

"Brandi," I repeated over and over again. She was the only person I could think of who had enough information on Seth, Justine, or me to pull all of this off.

"Damn!" I yelled to myself. "How could I have been so fucking trusting?"

I was fuming. I was angry. I was on the verge of crazy; then my phone rang.

"T'Shobi," the voice began, "have you arrived to your destination?"

"I'm pulling into the driveway now."

"Now, I need for you to stay and watch her reaction to what is revealed." The caller laughed before hanging up.

After looking at the time on the dashboard in my car, I realized that I almost missed the one-hour timeframe that was given to me. I sat in my car for a few moments before getting out. I was nervous. Knowing what had come to me in the same type of envelope, I was more than certain that she would have pictures of Seth and me, and just the thought of her discovering that was scary enough.

"This is becoming as bad as Atlanta," I said softly as I exited my car, still trying to understand why I chose not to leave.

"Who did you say this came from? Have you looked inside?" Justine asked me shortly after her mother let me in.

"Honestly, I don't know, Justine. I was just given instructions to bring this to you immediately."

I sat nervously as she slowly opened the envelope. I wasn't sure if I should begin walking out or running.

Justine began thumbing through each picture without any expression on her face. One time, she even seemed to have a smile on her face until—

"T'Shobi, how long have you and this Brandi *chick* been seeing each other?"

"Six months," I said softly.

"So, it's safe to assume you two are fucking?"

"Why do you ask?" I asked, losing eye contact, dropping my head down.

"I'm asking because if you two are fucking, then you are

aware of an extra tool she's carrying around, correct?" she asked while showing me a picture of Seth vividly sucking the part of Brandi that made her Brandon.

43

Justine

What I was looking at was definitely shocking as hell to me. I knew Seth had a lot of shit with him, and this one thing went way beyond the charts of what I had expected. But what got me the most was when I showed T'Shobi the picture of my husband sucking his "girlfriend's" extra body part, his reaction was not of surprise, but of shame.

"T'Shobi, is there anything you need to tell me?" I asked, more frustrated at the fact that he was gay, and not my missing husband.

"I . . . uhh . . . I think I need to leave now," he said as he got up from the chair he was sitting in.

"I think your ass need to stay here and tell me something, don't you?"

He stared at me long and hard, studying me to see what he should say or not say.

"It would take me twenty-seven years to explain my life to you, Justine," he said softly.

"I have a full day ahead of me. I'm waiting," I said right before his phone rang.

I watched him closely as he answered the phone. He mumbled "yes" and "mm-hmm" a few times, while nodding his head as if the person on the other end could actually see him. He then stopped, stared at me, and gave me his phone.

"Justine," a disguised voice began, "I wish I could see the look on your face now, but what I really would pay to see was the look on Seth's face this morning when he saw pictures of you and T'Shobi." The caller then gave a short and wicked laugh. "Yes, Justine, that's what I said, in case you misunderstood: Seth is still alive, and he knows about the affair between you and T'Shobi."

"Who is this?" I yelled. "What do you want?"

"What I want, you can't give to me," the voice said, becoming softer. "But for now, I have other plans for T'Shobi, so he must go. Please place him back on the phone."

I gave the phone back to T'Shobi and I watched him take instructions carefully. Once he hung up the phone, he remained seated for a few moments, staring at the floor.

"We need to talk," I said, making eye contact with him.

"We will, but first I have to deal with this." And with that, he was gone.

For the remainder of the day I couldn't remove the picture of Seth sucking on Brandi's dick. It was disgusting, but then I began to imagine T'Shobi doing the same thing to him—or her, or whatever it was. Then I thought about his passion and roughness for anal sex.

"Motherfucker!" I yelled out loud.

After my outburst, Janice walked in, looking at the pictures spread across my bed. As she examined each one, I watched her expressions, and received nothing.

"I told you that she wasn't what you thought she was," she said as she walked back out of door.

I suddenly remembered that earlier that week at church,

she had made the same comment. "Are you behind this?" I whispered, wondering if my baby sister knew more than what she was leading any of us to believe she knew.

44

Seth

I woke up drenched in sweat. Since receiving those pictures, my mind was in a whirlwind. I was fuming about what they portrayed. I still couldn't quite grasp the fact that Justine and T'Shobi were screwing each other. I had just settled the fact in my mind about him and Brandon, and now this.

I emerged from the couch, and every emotion I had experienced in those six months had finally grabbed on to me all at once, making me crazy. I began screaming for help, already knowing that in the past, these efforts went unheard; but it was all I knew to do, the only way I was given hope that somehow I would be rescued from this hell.

I paced back and forth as I rubbed all the hair on my face. It had just dawned on me that I hadn't shaved or even showered in months. If I smelled, my nose had become immune to the stench. Suddenly, I heard the chiming of a phone.

I stared at it long and hard, realizing that it hadn't been there before I had dozed off the last time.

"Hello?" I asked suspiciously.

An unknown voice spoke. "Good morning, Seth. How are you?"

"Who is this, and why do you have me trapped like this?"

"Patience, my friend, patience. Trust me. Time will reveal all," the voice cackled.

"I demand you tell me now who you are."

"Did you enjoy the photos?" the voiced asked, ignoring my command.

"I demand you release me now!"

"I wonder if you thought about which pictures I sent to Justine. The ones of you fucking T'Shobi in the ass, or the ones of you showing your delight in sucking Brandi—I mean Brandon's—dick?" the voice said before ending the call.

I stared at the phone after the call ended. My first reaction was to throw it; then it dawned on me. I could use it to call out.

I dialed the first number that came to mind.

"Hello," Justine said.

"Justine, this is Seth, I'm—" The call quickly dropped, and a wicked message took its place: "I'm sorry, but your pre-pay account has been expired. Please replenish your minutes using a valid credit card by pressing the pound key now."

45

TiTi

It felt great to breathe. Tinisha Jackson had finally left the building.

I was sitting in my cubicle at work when my cell phone began to vibrate.

"Speak to me."

"You need to explain yourself," Chase said.

"I beg your pardon?"

"You're screwing around with my brother? What kind of sick freak are you?" he said, full of pure anger.

"Well, my dear Chase, the jury is still out on the sick part, but I can more than assure you that I am a freak," I said, finding it difficult to control my laughter.

Before he could say another word, I clicked the END button then continued on with my current assignment—have lunch with my new best friend.

For weeks, I made myself friendly with T'Shobi's girlfriend at church. I knew the best way to get back at T'Shobi for what he did to Tinisha was to come in and sabotage whatever it was they had. I wasn't quite sure what I was going to do just yet, but I knew us becoming friends would get things started.

"Hey, girl," I said as Brandi walked into P.F. Chang's at Northlake Mall.

"Hey, Tinisha, how are you?" she said in her raspy voice.

"Glad to get away from the office and get something to eat," I said, smiling. "And, girl, we friends now. Call me TiTi."

After ordering our lunch, we sat for several moments, having idle conversations about this and that. We even talked about the mysterious disappearance of Pastor Reynolds.

"Do you think someone killed him and buried his body somewhere?" I asked.

My question must have done something to her, because suddenly a look of sadness appeared over her face.

"I don't know," she began, almost whispering, and slowly dropping her head. "I just hope all is okay with him."

"Did you know him?"

She slowly lifted her head back up and looked at me. I wasn't sure, but it appeared as if her eyes were watering.

"Yes, I do know him. I guess you could say he was a counselor." She paused to sip her tea. "In a sense, it was through him that I met T'Shobi."

As we were walking to our cars, her phone rang.

"Hey, babe," she said gleefully. "Just finished lunch with Tini—I mean TiTi. Hunh? Why? What's wrong? Okay, I'm on way. Will be there soon," she said right before giving me a quick good-bye then jumping into her Jaguar.

I knew something was wrong, so I did what I thought I should. I called the office to inform them that I was taking the afternoon off, and then I followed her to where she was going to meet her man, to see what I could do to help—all for Tinisha's sake, of course.

46

T'Shobi

When I left Justine's house, I rode around town for hours, trying to figure out who could have been behind all of this. It was driving me crazy. I wanted to do what I was used to, and that's run.

"Who could be doing this to me? And why?" I asked myself over and over again as I drove aimlessly through Charlotte.

About two hours into my drive, I found myself back at the same location where I received the pictures for Justine. I sat a distance up the street, away from the house, hoping to see someone come or go. For another two wasted hours, I saw nothing.

I finally decided to call Brandi to have her meet me at my place. She was still my number one suspect, and for whatever reasons, when she informed me that she was with Tinisha, my anger went into overdrive.

Before going home, I made two stops. The first was to the liquor store, and the second to my contact for some weed. My next assignment was not until the next morning, and I needed to wind down and try to come to the bottom of who was behind all of this.

***

"Why are you sitting with the lights off and the blinds closed in the daytime?" Brandi asked me as she walked into the smoke-filled room. "And how are you going to start a party without me?" she said as she walked toward me. She grabbed the perfectly rolled brown substance from my hand and took a hit.

"Since when did you start hanging with Tinisha?" I asked.

"Damn, this is good," she said after taking a long pull. "Who? Oh, TiTi. This was our first time actually hanging out, but we've been talking a lot on the phone over the past several weeks. She's a sweet girl."

"Do you know anything about these?" I asked, showing her the pictures I received the day before.

She studied them long and hard. I tried to study her expressions as she viewed them. I wasn't sure if I had gotten too high from the weed and liquor or what, but I could have sworn that she had a smile on her face.

"You know I know about your affairs. We talked about this, remember?"

"Fuck that. I'm talking about these pictures," I said, feeling my body tense up. "Do you know where the hell they came from?"

"I assume you took them."

Before I could stop myself, I knocked the shit out of Brandi.

"T'Shobi! What the hell is your problem?"

I hit her again.

"Justine received pictures of Seth sucking your dick. Now, I'm going to ask you again. Do. You. Know. Anything. About. These. Gotdamn pictures?" I shoved the pictures in front of her now bloody face.

Brandi looked at me in what looked like fear. I was hoping

to hell that she would fight back. In a mere matter of seconds, I felt everything that I'd ever felt in my lifetime rush through my body with a rage that truly scared the shit out of me.

"T'Shobi, I don't know a damn thing about any pictures," she said with sincerity.

A part of me believed it, but it wasn't enough to keep me from kicking her ass then sending her on her way.

After she left, I sat back on the floor and returned to what I was doing before she got there, then drifted off into my high.

"Hello," I said into the phone, angry about being awakened.

"T'Shobi, T'Shobi, T'Shobi. Now, why would you go and beat down a perfectly fine looking *wo-man* like that?" That damned disguised voice laughed into the phone. "I hope she heals soon, because I have plans for you, her, and me."

47

TiTi

I sat in my car in the parking lot of T'Shobi's apartment, prepared to sit there for hours. I had no idea why I was there or what I would accomplish, but something in me told me to just sit and wait.

Less than twenty minutes later, I saw Brandi running out of T'Shobi's house frantically. I wondered what was wrong. When she sped away in her car, I looked up at the window and saw him staring at her drive away while he guzzled what appeared to be an entire bottle of liquor.

After a few moments of watching him, I decided that I had better leave before he spotted me. As I drove home, I gave Brandi a call to see if I could pry information out of her.

"Hello." She sounded distraught.

"Hey, girl, I was just wondering if you wanted to go shopping or something this evening."

There was a long pause, and I could hear weakness in her voice.

"Not today, TiTi. I just need to go home and take a long, hot bath," she responded.

"Is everything all right?"

"T'Shobi and I just had a nasty fight, and I just need to go home and think about some things, that's all," she said with a sigh.

"You need me to come over? You wanna talk?"

Fifteen minutes later, I was pulling into the parking lot of her gated condominium complex in the SouthPark area of Charlotte. I had passed them several times before, and had wished I could afford to live there myself. To say that I was impressed was an understatement.

When she came to the door, she was wearing a pair of grey sweats and a burgundy Morehouse T-shirt.

"I've got wine and popcorn!" I said gleefully, raising the bag that contained the treats.

"Come in," she said as she quickly hid her face.

Once we walked into her living room, I noticed the fresh bruises on her face.

"What happened? Did T'Shobi do this to you?" I immediately became concerned.

I was shocked. I knew from my own experiences with him that he appeared to have a violent temper, but to strike a woman was something I never imagined he would do.

"TiTi," she began, "let's just enjoy the popcorn and wine, okay? I really don't want to talk about *him* right now," she stated as she sat down on the plush brown leather couch.

We sat for hours, watching movies and drinking while eating different types of snacks. She had more wine in the house, and before I knew anything, we had downed three bottles and were both feeling a little tipsy. I had forgotten that I was still in Tinisha's body, and wasn't quite used to drinking alcohol.

When I stood up, deciding that it was time for me to go home, I dropped right back down on the couch on top of Brandi. As I lay on top of her, our eyes met, and for the first time, I saw something different about her. I had never thought about being with a woman before, but in that moment, I found myself extremely attracted to her.

Before I could stop myself, my lips met hers. She received them openly and willingly, as she flipped me over, placing herself on top of me, continuing to kiss me as she caressed me gently. I welcomed it, enjoying every ounce of it, especially when she unbuttoned my pants and with one swift pull, had them, along with my panties, on the floor.

After sucking on my right breast, she then slowly moved further down until she met—

"Damn!" I screamed as she instantly made me orgasm.

Up until that point, Frederick was the only man I had been with that did it well, but Brandi did something that I could not even explain. She continued, never stopping, appearing to enjoy it more than me. Finally, she lifted her head and came back up to kiss me. I had no idea when she had become naked, but I was enjoying myself so much that it didn't bother me.

She kissed me hard, soft, hard again, then soft again, and I did the same back to her. Then . . .

"Wha-what is that?" I whispered in shock.

"TiTi, meet Brandon."

And she made my ass cum over and over again.

48

Justine

I debated with myself at least a thousand times about whether I should have informed anyone about my brief conversation with Seth. After making a couple of attempts to call the number back, only to get the same message about it being an expired prepaid account, I began to wonder if he was behind all of this himself.

I was at a point where nothing else that man did surprised or shocked me. For all I knew, he was behind all this picture foolishness. I was completely spent with him and all the years I'd wasted for reasons well beyond my own understanding.

There were a lot of answers that I needed to know, and although Seth carried many of those answers, I knew that he alone could not provide me those answers.

"Mama," I began as she walked in carrying a tray of food. "If I ask you something, will you be honest with me?"

"Of course I will, dear. I'm your mother."

For some strange and crazy reason, and it could have been because of all that had been going on over the past several months, or even several days, but I knew without a doubt I was about to explode.

"Go ahead, dear," she said, sensing my hesitation.

"Exactly how long have you known about Seth and Janice?"

She became nervous and uneasy. I could tell that my question was one that she wasn't prepared for.

"Now, I'm sure you have better things to think about than foolishness that transpired so many years ago," she said then got up from her chair and began picking up things and placing them back in the same exact spot.

"Mama, those things that happened so many years ago are creating turmoil now, so many years later."

"Baby, you need to get some rest," she said, ready to walk out of the door.

"Mama, look," I said, holding up the picture of Brandi and Seth. "Will you look at this? Seth is one sick pervert! For all I know, this fool could have molested my sons when they were young." I had become irate.

There was so much about that fool I had no knowledge of, and the sad thing about it was in his mess, I could vividly see my own. And it wasn't pretty either.

"Now, if you found out after I married him, then trust me, I understand," I said, pausing to take a sip of the water that was on my tray. "But if you knew what he had done to Janice before I married him..."

When she burst into tears and began praying into the air, I realized that my question had been answered.

"His father told me it was a stage that he would grow out of," she said through her tears.

"Mama, can you please leave now."

I was hoping that she wouldn't attempt to explain anything more. I was beyond any emotion, knowing that over thirty years ago, my mother knowingly placed me and my future in harm's way.

"Justine, things were different then. We thought problems like that were just minor stages," she said, pleading for me to understand.

"Minor?" I yelled. If I could have stood up and walked toward her, I would have slapped the shit out of my own mother.

"Mama, do you not realize the major damage that has been done to Janice? Do you not realize that fool's *minor* problem was a factor in why I despised my sister for so many years? Do you not realize the jeopardy placed on your entire family because of this?"

Her crying did not move me at all. In reality, it was beginning to piss me off.

"Mama, I think you better leave now before you see a tray of food flying your way," I said, feeling as if I were two seconds from losing my mind.

After she left the room, I needed to learn more things about my husband. I needed to find out who was behind these pictures, but being trapped in a bed, unable to move without assistance, I had to get in contact with the only person I knew who could help me at that moment.

"T'Shobi, as soon as you get this message, call me," I said on his voicemail.

49

T'Shobi

The sound of her voice was urgent, but I wasn't ready to face Justine yet. I was almost certain that she had discovered the affair between Seth and me by then, so I chose to remain on the floor, where I had been the entire night, doing what I knew best: hiding my problems.

I thought about going back to my contact and instead of buying my normal item, I would get something stronger that would take me away from this world.

I listened to her message three more times and thought about shutting my phone off, but remembered that I was waiting on the call to begin my journey for my next mission.

What I had done to Brandi played with me from the time she left until that very moment. I was finally certain, after showing her the pictures, that she had nothing to do with it; however, I was angry and scared, and she was the closest person around to vent that frustration.

After showering and sobering up the best I could, I grabbed my keys and waited for the call that would tell me when to begin my next mission. This was definitely a mission that had me more nervous than having to deliver the pictures to Justine.

"As you walk out your door," the voice began when it finally called me back. "You will see yet another envelope. This one is for the administrative board of the church. They are meeting in exactly one hour." The voice then paused.

I sat waiting for further instruction. I began to think that the call had ended and my instructions had been given.

"Sorry," the voice said, returning. "You are to give this package to Deacon Malachi Barber, understood?"

"Yes," I said.

"Oh, I forgot to tell you. You have no worries. This package does not contain any *questionable* pictures featuring you this time." The voice laughed before ending the call.

When I arrived at the church, I sat in my car. I was tempted to open the package to view it for myself, but I was afraid. There were just too many uncertainties. I was still trying to figure out what would happen if they asked me where it came from. Because I had no definite answers myself, they would have no choice but to believe that I was the one responsible.

"Brother Wells, what brings you here so early on a Thursday morning?" Deacon Barber asked as he presented his hand for me to shake.

"Well," I said, pausing, trying to come up with a reason I had the package to eliminate any suspicion. "This package addressed to the administrative board somehow got mixed up with some of the music department's mail, and I just wanted to get it to you as soon as possible."

"Well, thank you, son," he said, examining the package. "Well, you have a blessed day." With that said, he walked into the church, while at the same time opening the package.

I began searching the parking lot to see if anyone was looking. Since the call I received after Brandi left the house, my mind went into overdrive, thinking about being followed. I was one hundred percent sure that whoever was behind this was somewhere near.

As I continued to search the area, I thought I saw a suspicious car; then my phone rang. I looked at the caller ID, and although I didn't want to answer, I knew that I would have to speak to her eventually.

"Justine," I said, answering the phone.

"Did you not get my message? When I said call me as soon as you got that message, I meant right then, not later."

"I just got it," I said, lying.

"I need for you to come to my house. Are you able to do that now? If not, you definitely need to make yourself available, understood?" she said, ending the call.

50

Justine

"Who does that fool think he's dealing with?" I said to myself, hanging up the phone.

"Who are you talking to, Justine?" Janice said, walking into the room.

"None of your damned business," I responded, now mad at everyone.

Since the conversation with my mother the day before, I had been full of nothing but hurt, anger, and disgust. I just couldn't believe that in thirty years of marriage, although knowing about his other activities, this totally flew right over my head.

"Did you know Seth was into men?" I asked Janice.

After my small explosion with her, she was heading back out of the door, but stopped.

"No, I didn't, but I don't put anything past his trifling ass," she said matter-of-factly.

"Did you know Mama knew what Seth was doing to you?"

She walked back into the room and sat down in the chair closest to me. For several moments, she remained silent. Suddenly, my heart softened, and I placed my own personal victimization aside.

"Janice, I'm sorry for going off a few moments ago." I

reached out for her hand. "I'm sure you went through a lot."

Although she told me all of what she chose to remember of being offended by that dog, she really didn't have to say anything with words. Her tears told it all.

T'Shobi arrived to the house exactly twenty-four minutes from the time I called him. When my mother escorted him in, my eyes were so focused on her that I initially didn't notice he walked in with another envelope. Somehow, I was hoping that she was standing close by when Janice told me what she could of being molested.

"Come in, T'Shobi. Have a seat," I said, directing him to the chair on the opposite side of the bed. "Have you met my sister, Janice?"

"Yes," he responded softly.

The look on his face was hard for me to decipher. After he and Janice gave a short greeting, she then left, closing the door behind us.

"Do you have any idea who could be behind this?" I asked, cutting straight to the chase.

"No . . . Yes . . . No . . . Ye—Hell, Justine, I really don't know. I'm totally confused right now."

Once again, I studied his face, looking for something, and again I saw nothing.

"What do you know about this Brandi *chick?*"

"I thought I had gotten to know her well. She seemed to be someone I could trust."

"But now?"

"I don't know," he said, slightly shrugging his shoulders.

"Are you on the DL?" I asked.

With that question, he looked directly into my eyes, finally giving me something other than that solemn look he walked in with.

"Justine, I know before that I mentioned to you briefly about my past, growing up in foster care, and even being placed in a juvenile facility." He paused, giving a slight cough. "But it actually goes a little deeper."

He paused yet again. It appeared as if he was thinking of what to say.

I wanted to tell him to hurry the hell up, but when I looked at him, I could see the same exact look on his face that I saw on Janice's.

"I was molested by my adoptive mother when I was ten." His eyes began to get watery. "When her husband, who was a pastor, caught us, she cried rape. I was sent to a facility, where I was abused by other boys for nine months, until it was discovered that she lied."

Suddenly, my heart dropped. I began to see him as the little boy with the curly hair and grayish-blue eyes getting picked on, not the sick down low brother that, if I could move normally, was on the verge of getting his ass kicked.

"When I was released, I went to stay with a very nice lady, and for months, we lived in her house together; then her son, Russell, came to stay with us when he got out of jail. I was almost sixteen, and he was thirty." He paused. "He was the first person that made me feel as if I was loved."

We sat in silence. I began to understand his roughness when he and I had sex. He was angry, and while with me, he punished me. When I started thinking about our age difference, I knew that in his eyes, I was nothing more than the woman who victimized him.

I felt hurt for him. I felt hurt for Janice. Although I, too, was a victim of Seth's antics, mine carried little to no weight compared to what the both of them had endured for a life-time.

After telling me of his confusion throughout his life on his sexuality, and that being with Brandi was the closest thing to understanding himself he had ever been, he got up from the chair, gave me the envelope that he walked in with, then left.

As I sat in my room in complete silence, I knew that everything I had heard that day was more than I had actually expected. The goal I had set out for that morning was to raise hell with everyone who came into my presence. I wanted everyone to pay for what was happening in my life. I felt that I deserved sympathy, and was going to demand that I got it

I cried for twenty minutes as I sat alone in my room. Although it was sunny and bright, darkness was all I saw. After getting myself together, I decided to open the envelope.

"What the fuck?" I asked after viewing pictures of Seth and T'Shobi together.

51

TiTi

It seemed as if I awakened before my eyes opened. I began thinking about the strange dream I had just had, then I opened my eyes and realized that I was not home sleeping in my bed, and what I thought happened in a dream was reality.

"Good morning," Brandi said, walking into the room wearing a black silk robe that showed her breasts, and carrying two ceramic mugs steaming at the top.

I finally understood the reason her voice was raspy. She really wasn't a she, but a he that looked like one.

"Damn," I said as I extended both hands to accept the warm substance she made.

"I'm sorry, TiTi. I should have told you," she said.

"Damn," I repeated.

"Things just happened so quickly, and the moment seemed so right."

"Damn." I couldn't stop myself.

"And if you are wondering, yes, T'Shobi knows."

"Damn."

"TiTi, I really do apologize, but even after you found out, you didn't stop me," she said with her eyes never leaving mine.

"Damn."

"TiTi, can you say anything other than *damn*?" she asked.

"Can we do it one more time before I go?"

"Damn," Brandi said.

52

T'Shobi

When I walked out of Justine's bedroom, I bumped into her sister, who had apparently been standing at the door the entire time, listening.

"Excuse me," I said as I continued my way through the house.

"T'Shobi," she said before taking a long pause. "I'm sorry about what happened to you." She began crying.

As I drove home, the tears that I held while at Justine's came down rushing nonstop. She was the third person I'd told about my life. I wasn't sure what the voice had in mind for me, but I knew I had to show Justine the pictures of Seth and me before I was instructed to do so. I viewed telling her my life story, although I was taking a chance, as a way of giving her a better understanding of me.

I tried calling Brandi twice and received no answer. I thought about leaving her a voice message, but the apology she deserved from me needed to be done face to face. I didn't expect her to accept it, but it was something I had to do to ease my own pain for what I had done to her.

Since I couldn't get her on the phone, I decided to drive

to her place. The designated spot for her visitor was already occupied. When I saw the car that was parked in the spot, I recognized it immediately, and decided to leave. I knew they had become close over the past several weeks, but for Tinisha to be at her house at eleven o'clock in the morning was strange to me. Without adding more questions to mind that was full of them, I turned around and decided to make my two favorite stops to get my two favorite items and go home.

"Hello," I answered.

"Baby, this is MeeMa. How are you this morning?"

"I'm here, MeeMa," I said still feeling the high I had been on for the last forty-eight hours. I'd bought a double amount of what I normally did, to add with what I had left from my previous purchases, then passed out. I was so out of it that I didn't realize that two days had passed by.

"You don't sound well. Are you okay?"

I wanted to tell her yes, but she knew me well enough to know that I wasn't.

"No, ma'am, I'm not. I have a lot of things going on," I said.

"You should come home for a visit. I will pay for it."

"That's okay, MeeMa. If I came, you know I wouldn't need your help," I said, feeling a smile come across my face for the first time in a week.

"I know you can, but I want to see you. Do you realize it's been almost two years?"

She was right. The last time I saw her was when she came to visit when I bought my house in Atlanta, a house that was now sitting empty.

"MeeMa, why don't you and Roscoe move into the house in Atlanta? He can go to Clark, or even Morehouse."

"Baby, that's your house for when you decided to settle and lay some real roots." She paused. "Besides, I need to be here for Russell."

Where I had finally begun to feel a little sunshine, her mentioning Russell brought the clouds back.

"How is Russell doing?"

"He gave his soul to the Lord. That's all that matters now," she said softly.

Russell contracted HIV five years earlier, and due to an on again, off again drug addiction, it had recently turned to full-blown AIDS. I'd often wondered if he had it when he arrived home from prison, but I never tried to place much emphasis on it.

"You really should consider a visit soon," she said, breaking me away from my daze.

"I am in the middle of a project now, MeeMa, but I will definitely consider a visit soon."

After I hung up with her, the phone rang again before I could lay it down.

"Hmm, we missed church today, I see," the voice said, reminding me what day of the week it was.

"Who is this? I'm getting sick of the games!"

"T'Shobi, I sense you are getting agitated," the voice mocked.

"Just so you know, I've already shown Justine the pictures of Seth and me."

There was a long pause.

"Hello?" I said.

"Thanks. That was actually your next assignment."

There was a long silence.

"I really wish you had gone to church today, T'Shobi. I would have loved to have been at New Deliverance myself just to hear the buzz that's going around about the package you delivered."

I had almost forgotten about the package. Suddenly, I began to get nervous.

"What was in it?" I asked.

"You should have been there to find out for yourself," the voice said, laughing.

"Who are you, and why are you doing this?"

"Patience, T'Shobi, patience. Once I return to Charlotte tomorrow, I will call you with your next assignment," the voice said then hung up.

"So, you are not always in Charlotte?" I whispered as I continued staring at the phone.

53

Seth

There was another package waiting for me when I woke up. When I opened this one, I knew that even if I physically survived this ordeal, my life was still over.

The documents that sat in front of me would not only shame my family, they could also place me in jail for a very long time. I studied the package over and over, hoping to find any clue about who was behind all of this, but I found nothing.

"Who in the hell is doing this?" I asked myself.

I was mad with confusion, and just wondered if this was the wrath that God was placing on me. My life was a lie, and my death would reveal all of my nasty truths.

As I cried out, the prepaid phone that was left for me days before began to ring. I hadn't heard from whoever was behind this since that day.

"Hello," I said angrily into the phone.

"Greetings, Seth. I hope that all is well with you today," the person on the other end said with a chuckle.

"Who the hell are you?" I asked.

"So, what did you think of the package?"

"How did you gain this information?"

"I wonder what went through Deacon Barber's mind when he examined the documents."

Suddenly, I knew my life was over. This was definitely my end.

"You damned son-of-a-bitch, who the fuck are you?"

"Seth, is that any way to talk to the person who literally holds your life in their hand? I'm sure you were taught better than that."

"When I get out of here, you better hope that I never find you, because you are dead!" I said.

"Seth, Seth, Seth, never make promises that you can't keep."

I was beginning to feel weak and powerless; if I had ever felt that way before, it was so long ago that I had no idea what it felt like until that moment.

"Why are you doing this to me?" I asked.

"You took something that belonged to me," the person answered before hanging up.

54

Justine

Since T'Shobi had given me the pictures three days ago, my emotions were mixed. I cried, I screamed, I cursed, I cried some more, and then I became agitated. All of the things that had taken place over the past several months seemed to be too unreal. It was as if I were living a real life soap opera.

I needed to get out and move around. I was trapped, and along with all the foolishness that was going on, it was damn near driving me insane.

"Can I get you something?" my mother asked, sticking her head in the door.

For days since our conversation, although she maintained her distance, she still made attempts to talk to me. They were attempts that I made sure were unsuccessful. For me, she was still partly to blame for what was going on, and because of her part in this, she definitely lost my trust.

I dialed T'Shobi's number several times during the day, but I knew that I needed time. Part of me wanted to curse him out, and there was a part of me that wanted to console him. It was strange that I felt sorry for my lover, who was also one of my husband's lovers as well. Like I said, this was one big-ass real life soap opera.

Several times I thought about using the pills that sat on the table beside my bed, as a way to end this drama, but I knew that would create more embarrassment to my family. I needed to find a way to stay strong and fight this evil that clouded us for over thirty years.

When my mother returned, I had all the pictures that were brought to me throughout the week spread across the bed.

"Justine, Deacon Barber is here to see you."

As I began to gather the pictures and place them back in the envelope, I couldn't help but wonder why he came to the house to see me. Once I was ready to see him, I informed my mother.

"Justine, how are you?" he asked as he walked in carrying yet another envelope.

"I guess I'm making it. Please have a seat."

For moments, he only stared at me and then the floor, as if he was trying to gather the right words to say.

"What can I do for you, Malachi?" I asked, breaking the deafening silence.

"First, let me say that I apologize for not coming to see you more since your accident." He paused then looked back to the floor. "Secondly, I apologize for showing up unannounced and with the questions I'm about to ask."

It appeared that more bad news was about to rear its damned head.

"What is it, Malachi?"

"Do you know . . ." He paused again. "We came across some information. The information suggests many improprieties on the part of Seth. I have to take this information to the police, due to his absence, and I wanted to give you the heads up, as well as ask if you knew anything about it."

As I read through the information from his envelope, as with all of the previous ones, it left me realizing I had been living with a complete stranger my entire adult life.

55

TiTi

I woke up to Lil Wayne blasting from my radio. I didn't know the song or even understand what he was saying, but the beat of hip-hop was a new turn-on for me. It made me feel free, and made my body move in ways that I had never known possible.

Tinisha's mother would have died if she saw the way the shell of her daughter had been acting. The things that she had been protected from all her life were now a complete part of it.

I couldn't believe how much I had missed in life. The music, the dancing, the partying—all of it was great, but what I loved the most was the sex. Sex had almost been part of my everyday need since the first time I was with Malik.

Although he was good the first three times, because I wanted T'Shobi to be my first, Malik never scratched that itch that needed scratching. Frederick was actually great, but he didn't fulfill that need either. It was not until my adventure with Brandi that I actually felt satisfied. When she tasted me, I began feeling things that seemed unnatural. I couldn't believe that a woman was actually doing that to me, but when I discovered her secret, although surprised, I was a little bit disappointed.

I never thought that I was attracted to women, and honestly, my upbringing had me so far in the left field that if there was an attraction, I would have run and prayed. But, although she was a man that looked like a woman, Brandi definitely piqued my curiosity for the *real* thing.

After showering and getting ready for work, I checked my phone for messages.

"Como se miota shamba shey. Como se miota shamba shey," I heard my mother praying to my voicemail.

I immediately hit the delete button. I knew that eventually I would have to talk with her, but it definitely wasn't going to be that morning.

"Hey, Tinisha," one of the young attorneys said as I walked in the door. "You are looking real good this morning,"

"Thanks, Bill. I appreciate that."

"Would you like to do lunch sometime?"

His question did something to me, and before my brain had a conversation with my mouth, I said something that I instantly knew would be another groundbreaking experience.

"Do you want to have lunch sometime, or fuck sometime, Bill?"

His face turned so red that I forgot he was white. He began to stare at me long and hard, as if he were deciphering if I were joking or serious.

"And if I said fuck?" he responded.

"How much are you willing to pay?"

"How much are you worth?" he responded quickly.

"Well, my dear, if you have to ask, then obviously you can't afford me," I said, smiling. "I tell you what. When you have what you would consider to be a decent offer, you know where to find me." And with that, I walked to my cubicle to begin my day.

About fifteen minutes before my lunch break, I saw Bill slowly walking toward my area. When he made it to my desk, he handed me a folder as if he were handing me work. After he walked away, I opened it, discovering a small envelope with *Marriott* and a handwritten number on it. There was also a white bank envelope containing twenty one-hundred dollar bills.

56

T'Shobi

Another week had passed by, and I still hadn't talked with Brandi since our altercation. I tried calling her a few more times, but she never answered the phone, and she refused to return my calls.

I was beginning to believe that maybe that was the best thing for both of us. As much as I tried to make what we had seem right, I knew that it wasn't. My life was altered years ago, and instead of changing, I attempted to adapt to it. Adapting was the reason I always found myself in crazy situations.

It had also been a week since I heard from the voice, and that made me extremely nervous. When I discovered that the package that I was instructed to give to the church administrative board contained information on Seth embezzling several million dollars over the years— buying expensive automobiles, condominiums, and even a house for his lovers—I was almost certain that whomever was behind the voice had access to a lot of information on a lot of people.

Earlier in the week, I visited the church to speak to Deacon Barber about resigning. He appeared to be genuinely sincere about not wanting to accept my resignation. He even asked if I could stay and help while they located someone to replace me. I wanted to say no to the request, but realized that I still needed something to occupy my mind.

***

The voice had yet to bring forth any information about me to others. From the way it appeared, the main focus was set strictly on Seth. I began wondering what kind of person Seth really was. I thought about the many conversations we had before, when he showed me love. It appeared to be the same love that I felt from Russell, but I began to realize that any love from anyone, man or woman, was false.

I had also come to the realization that my life might never be easy and simple, and I might never get a chance at normalcy.

I thought about my last visit with Justine. I wanted to call her after leaving the pictures, and was surprised when I didn't hear from her immediately. Knowing her the way I thought I did, I was more than certain that she had questions, as well as a few choice words to express her disdain. But what I received was something unexpected.

"How long were you two . . . fucking?" she asked solemnly.

"It started around the same time as you and I did."

Silence.

"He came on to you?" she asked.

"Yes, he did."

"Did you do him, or he just did you, or both?" she spoke softly.

"Both," I responded almost in a whisper.

More silence.

"What attracted you to him?"

I remained silent. That was a question that, although I knew the answer, the more I thought about it, I began to wonder if it really made sense.

My attraction for men started with Russell. It was not what most attractions were based on. It wasn't driven on looks, or even sexual desires, but from my own personal desire to be loved.

I did my best to explain that to her. I wanted her to understand my life the way I saw it. Women, older women, deceived me. Mrs. Pratt was my first real encounter with a woman, and her actions created something in me that triggered a hate.

"So, you hated me?" she asked after my long explanation.

"No, I didn't hate you. I guess it was more or less you represented something that I saw as a threat," I said, unsure if she understood.

"The last time we had sex . . ." she said, pausing. "You forced yourself in me. Was that punishment from what Mrs. Pratt did to you?"

"Yes," I said solemnly.

The remainder of that conversation mostly dealt with the situation at hand. I told her that it was difficult to identify who could be behind this, because it appeared that everything coming out in the public mostly dealt with Seth and his indiscretions.

"That could be any damn body," she responded.

"He has that many enemies?"

"Seth has done a lot of dirty things to a lot of people," she responded with anger.

"I'm getting nervous, Justine," I said. "I haven't heard from the person behind all of this in a week."

Before hanging up the phone, we agreed to communicate daily. We also decided that it was time to put our own plans into action. If we wanted to find out who was behind this, we were going to have to make the next move.

57

Justine

"Have you heard from Jonathan?" I asked Janice when she walked into my room with my breakfast.

"No. Why do you ask?"

"Just curious to know," I said, looking directly into her eyes.

"You think he has something to do with this, don't you?"

"What do you think, Janice? Do you think he's capable of all of this?"

She sat down in the chair and began crying. "I don't know," she whispered.

"How long has he known who is father is?"

She went on to tell me that he had started asking her questions around the age of six, and he also asked a lot of questions as to why they never visited family. Around the age of twelve, he took a strong interest in computers, and had actually become well versed in using the Internet as a vital tool to gain knowledge. On his own, he found out who his father was.

"For months, he wouldn't speak to me," she said, still crying. "He just couldn't understand how I could sleep with my sister's husband."

"I can imagine that hurt you."

"Justine, you just don't know the half." She paused. "I eventually had to tell him when the *relationship* began, and his anger redirected toward Seth."

After her story, I was speechless. Again I began to get angry about how one act many years ago had created so much pain to a small group of people. I also realized that Seth was a bigger bastard than I had already known him to be.

"He's very wealthy," she started again.

I was initially confused about who she was talking about.

"He embezzled the money from the church," I said with disdain.

"No, I'm talking about Jonathan." She looked up at me, wiping away her tears. "When I said that he became very knowledgeable about computers, I mean he became extremely knowledgeable. He learned how to use it for more than just finding Seth."

She stood up then walked to the window, a place in the room I noticed that she went to a lot over the past several days.

"He created a Web site that searched for deadbeat parents, and eventually sold it two years ago for millions. He's been taking very good care of me; even had me committed into one of the best rehab facilities in the country."

Suddenly, it hit me. All of the information received could have come from him. He had the knowledge, and apparently the money, to do any and all of this.

After my conversation with her, I immediately called T'Shobi and told him all that was explained to me.

"We need to find your nephew," he said with desperation.

Although I agreed, something still told me that he was not the creator of all of this havoc.

58

Seth

"I took something that belonged to you?" I repeated the same thing over and over for days. It was the last thing that my captor said to me, and the only thing that chose to stay in my head.

I was beginning to believe that I had finally lost my mind. I had been in seclusion from the world for what seemed like an eternity, and it had taken a toll on me. At one point, I stopped eating and drinking, hoping that I would wither away and die, but just when I vowed to not eat or drink, my desire to know who was doing this and why overwhelmed me. I had to live, at least until I knew.

I got up from the couch and walked to the tiny bathroom that was provided for me. I looked in the mirror and saw a monster. I hadn't shaved since being there, and my hair had grown out into an uneven afro.

"You look bad," I said to myself. "And you stink."

There were no hygiene products available to me; no comb, toothpaste, or soap. All I had were my thoughts and those damned envelopes, along with a phone that only worked when I was called by whomever had done this dreadful thing.

That time in seclusion did nothing but drive me deeper

and deeper into insanity. I had too much time to think, not only about my current situation, but about my actions of the past. Peace was never with me. When I was awake, I had those pictures and documents of me taking money from the church, to haunt me during the day. When I slept, I had visions of what I had done to Janice to haunt me in my sleep.

Thoughts of my childhood danced around, and for the first time, I came to some sort of understanding about why I did the things that I did.

Growing up, my self-esteem was very low. I was always afraid to talk to girls my age for fear of rejection. If it had not been for Justine's aggressiveness or our families putting us together, I never would have had enough nerve to talk to her.

When I would visit their home and see Janice running around playing, I watched her. I was always attracted to the younger girls in the neighborhood and at church. I didn't understand why, and when I tried to talk to my father about it, he only dismissed it as a phase I would get through. Then something happened one day that changed me forever.

It was a Saturday afternoon at Justine's grandmother's house. She and I were sitting on the couch in the living room, watching *Soul Train*, when Janice walked in and sat on my lap. I couldn't control what was going on in my body. My emotions went haywire, and before I knew it, I jumped up, pushing her off of me. I ran to the bathroom to relieve myself. From that point on, every chance she got, she ran to sit on my lap.

I felt she knew what she was doing. She had to have known that she was turning me on, because for weeks, my reaction was always the same. Then one day, when we were alone in one of the Sunday school rooms in the back of the church, it happened, and continued to happen for years.

Maybe I should have known better, but for thirty years, I believed only one thing: she knew what she was doing.

59

TiTi

In less than two days, I had discovered a new power: the power my sweetness had to make men pay for it.

Bill returned to my desk for the next two days, carrying a similar folder with the same contents. In less than a week's time, I had made two months in salary off of him. Honestly, the sex with him was horrible, but he more than compensated with the money.

"Was it as good for you as it was for me?" he asked after the third *date*.

"Better, I'm sure," I responded, thinking about the money in my pocketbook as I dressed.

"One day we are really going to have that lunch," he said with a goofy smile.

"Trust me, baby, you are feeding me well," I said as I sashayed my way out the door and back to the office as if nothing had happened.

I knew that if he paid, there were more that would do the same. I was ready to incorporate my new fun into a prosperous venture.

"You want me to give you how much?" Chase questioned.

His lame ass wanted me, and I refused to continue giving him what he wanted for free. He was not worth the time.

"You heard me. Three thousand dollars," I said, staring him directly in his face.

"Tinisha, I don't have that kind of money to just give you. I have a wife and kids."

"Oh, well," I said, walking toward the entrance of the church.

"Tinisha, wait," he said with desperation. "I will see what I can do. Can we meet up Wednesday after work?"

"As long as you have what I ask for. And how many times do I need to remind you that my name is TiTi?" I said, walking away.

When I finally made my way inside the church, it was packed as usual. Since the disappearance of Pastor Reynolds, it seemed as if people were coming from all over the place, mainly to see if there were any developments in his strange and abrupt absence.

Somewhere deep inside, I could feel Tinisha's presence in me, trying to resurface, especially when T'Shobi was nearby; but I knew I couldn't let her come back. I knew I had to continue to suppress her. She had to remember why she brought me out. It was because of him.

T'Shobi was the first man Tinisha wanted, and the first man to turn her down. Tinisha brought me out to help build the confidence that he destroyed.

After church, I "accidently" bumped into him as he was leaving.

"I hear you like to do it in the butt," I said with a smirk. "If I tooted up, would you do me?"

He stared at me for a moment with a look that could kill. I could hear Tinisha deep within, crying for him, wanting to tell him that she was sorry for the things I was saying. But I held her down.

"Go to hell," he whispered as he walked away.

I laughed as I saw him get into his car.

"Do you have plans for the afternoon?" Bill asked.

As soon as I got in my car to leave the church, he called my cell.

"As a matter of fact, I do," I lied.

"I was hoping to get a chance to spend a little more quality time with you."

Spending quality time with him was definitely not in my plans. The two thousand he had given me each time was for one hour and one hour only.

"I'm sorry, Bill, but I have already made these plans, and I really can't break them."

"I will give you six thousand dollars right now if I could see you," he said.

"What time and where?"

One thing I discovered quickly: my *good* pussy could make a man play a tune that would have me dancing like Beyoncé only wished she could.

60

T'Shobi

I wanted to strangle the shit out of Tinisha for the comment she made to me. She said it loud enough for people who were walking past us to hear. It took all of me to hold myself back and not repeat on her what had happened to Brandi.

Although I didn't consider myself to be a violent person, I'd found myself unable to control my temper, especially with all that had happened in the previous weeks. The past few days alone had been a continuation of more hell, and I was really mad that I accepted Deacon Barber's request for me to stay until they could find a replacement.

When I finally made it to my car, for reasons I couldn't explain, I looked back and saw Tinisha still staring at me with that wicked and cynical smile.

"Crazy bitch," I whispered to myself.

As soon as I sat in my car, my phone began to ring.

"Good afternoon, T'Shobi," the voice said.

I remained silent. It had been days since we last spoke, and even in that conversation, it was quite vague.

"Are we playing silence today?"

I still remained quiet.

"Actually, I really don't need for you to say a word." The voice paused. "Tomorrow, I will need for you to return to the house I sent you to a few weeks ago. There, you will find yet another package that I would like for you to deliver. I will call you first thing in the morning with the details."

Before I could respond, the caller hung up. I remained in my car in the parking lot of the church for ten minutes before driving away. My heart was pumping with energy, and my hands were sweaty. My body temperature felt as if it was rising, and my temples began to beat as if they were going to jump out of my head.

I called Justine to inform her of the conversation, and I immediately began to wonder again if her nephew was responsible. From the story she told me, it just made sense to me that he could be the one responsible for all of this. He was the product of a crazy situation, produced by what appeared to be an unstable man. I knew firsthand what effect the actions of one person could have on others.

It hurt that I had actually begun to trust and have feelings for Seth. I couldn't explain what it was, or even why I felt the way I did about him, but once discovering what he had done to Janice years ago, similar to what Mrs. Pratt did to me, I wished that he was somewhere nearby so I could destroy him my damn self.

"Where is this house?" Justine asked.

"It's in a moderate neighborhood on the south side of Charlotte. Not fancy or glamorous."

"Take a picture of it so I can see," she instructed.

The next morning, I was up early, anticipating the call from the voice. After showering, I sat on the couch with my phone in my hand, ready to leave when I got the call. Once again, the thoughts of who was behind all of this crept through my mind. There were several individuals over the years affected by Seth's actions, so the process of elimination had been difficult.

"The package is waiting for you," the voice said when I finally got the call.

"Who is this?" I asked, hoping to finally receive some type of clue.

"You will know in time, T'Shobi," was my response before the voice ended the call.

When I arrived at the house, I decided to walk around it, with hopes of gaining some type of clue.

I peeked through the windows and saw nothing but an empty inside. I walked to the back of the house and saw nothing but an empty yard. As I was about to return to the front porch, I noticed steps that descended, as if to a basement.

When I got closer to the bottom of the steps, I noticed that the window was covered.

"Damn," I whispered to myself.

When I walked back to the front of the house and picked up the package, my phone rang.

"I see that the curiosity is really killing you, isn't it?" The voice laughed then quickly hung up.

I returned to my car and noticed that the package had Justine's sister's name on it, once again leaving me completely clueless as to who was behind this.

61

Justine

The three of us sat quietly in the living room at my house, staring at the package with Janice's name on it. My mother had initially joined us, but as she watched the look in her younger daughter's eyes, I could tell that the pain of thirty years had finally caught up with her.

"Have you talked to your son?" T'Shobi asked, finally breaking the silence.

She said nothing, only shook her head.

"Do you want me to open it?" I asked her as I saw her hands trembling.

"No, I can do it," she whispered.

We watched her as she used a letter opener to slowly cut through it. Before completely opening it, she stopped.

"Jonathan said he has nothing to do with this," she said. "I don't understand why whoever is behind this is sending me something."

I continued to watch her, holding back the anger I had for the person responsible for this. Janice had already been through so much in life. For her life to be subjected to the same ridicule we had been through was, in my opinion, downright evil.

She emptied the contents of the envelope onto the table. It was a letter and what appeared to be a house key.

"Janice," she began reading almost in a whisper, "I am truly sorry for all that you have endured in your lifetime. It is not my intent to include you in this, but I need for you to hold on to this key, and when the time is appropriate, I will give you further instructions."

Immediately after Janice finished reading the letter, T'Shobi's phone rang.

"Hello," he answered. "Yes, I understand."

"What did they say?" I asked.

"The voice told me to stay calm and that all of this will be over soon."

"That was it?" I asked, confused.

He nodded his head and then left.

For the remainder of the day, I watched Janice walk through the house in a complete daze. A few times, she attempted to make calls to Jonathan, leaving him countless messages to return the calls, but he never did.

Later in the evening, I called my two sons over. For weeks, I held off from telling them all that was going on, but I knew that with the discovery of Seth's embezzlement, it would not be much longer before his other indiscretions came to the light.

"I don't believe it," Chase said. "Dad is not like that. He's not gay!"

When I showed them the pictures of Seth and Brandi, Frederick stood up and balled his fists. As he walked toward

the door, he hit the wall so hard that he created a hole. Chase
remained in the chair beside me, staring at the pictures.

"Isn't that T'Shobi's girlfriend?" he asked.

"She was his girlfriend," I responded solemnly.

62

Seth

"What do you want? I will give you whatever you need. Just let me leave," I pleaded to the person on the other line.

Another week had gone by, and I was still trapped like an animal. The person on the other end of the phone constantly called the phone that was left for me. I continued to try not to eat the food or drink the water that was left for me, because I was more than certain that something was placed inside them that made me sleep.

"What did I do?"

"How many times must I tell you, Seth? You took something of mine, and I intend to get it back."

Once they ended the call, I remained on the couch, staring at the glare of the TV. Again, I remained paralyzed by my situation.

"Prison would be better than this," I said to myself before drifting back to sleep.

When I woke up again, there was a suit bag lying across the floor, with a travel bag next to it. On top of the bag was a short note: *The time is near.*

63

TiTi

"Tinisha, what has gotten into you, child? I did not raise you to talk to me that way."

Tinisha's mother and I had been on the phone for nearly twenty minutes, and I was surprised that I allowed the conversation to last that long.

"Bitch, how many times must I explain to you that I am not your daughter?"

"Como se miota shamba shey. Como se miota shamba shey."

"I don't have time for this shit," I said before finally ending the call.

It was hard for me to get people to understand that the Tinisha Jackson that everyone once knew was no longer alive. TiTi had taken her place, and TiTi was going to remain. There were many times that I could hear Tinisha cry to come out, but that heifer could not come back and ruin what I had created.

Life was good, and life I knew was about to get even that much more grand. I was experiencing a new life, one that provided me with the pleasures and treasures I had never imagined.

***

After spending that Sunday evening with Bill, I called Brandi to see if she wanted to go and splurge a little bit off of what I made. When I arrived at her house, we sat around for a few moments, talking.

After I explained to her what had led me to become who I was, her eyes softened, and they even seemed to show an understanding.

"We all have a first that does something in our lives that helps to create the person that we become," she said.

Before leaving her place to go to The Jazz Café, I asked her a question that I had been dying, yet afraid, to ask since meeting her.

"What do you do for a living?"

Her eyes gleamed and her lips began to curl into a small smile.

"Let's just say I am a dirty little secret," she said, grabbing her purse and instructing me to head to her Jaguar.

That night, she introduced me to just about everybody who was anybody in the club. There were a few professional athletes there that knew her by name, and a few even made passes at me.

I felt comfortable, and I felt free. It felt that another new world had begun to open up right in my face.

"Hello, beautiful," a tall, chocolate brother said to me as he handed me a glass of wine. "My name is Corey Dice. I play for the Charlotte Wildcats."

"What's a Charlotte Wildcat?" I asked, dumbfounded.

His toothy grin turned me on, and I began to find myself getting moist.

"Would you like to dance?"

"No, I want to fuck. Now!"

***

The next morning, I woke up beside him in his mini mansion right outside of Charlotte in South Carolina.

"Good morning," he said as he woke up.

I'll be damned if he wasn't still looking good and turning me on even more.

"Can I get you anything?" he asked sincerely.

"I think I'm going to need a ride to my car. It's still at my girlfriend's house," I responded softly.

He rose from the bed and walked over to his dresser, picked up a key ring, and removed one key.

"Here, take my Porsche. You can bring it back to me tonight."

On my way back to Brandi's house, I called work to let them know that I was sick and had to take the day off. I then called Brandi to let her know I was on my way back to her place. When I got there, I saw one of the guys who I met the night before leaving.

"Does he know about—" I asked her when I walked in.

"Yep."

"Is that what you mean by being a dirty li'l secret?"

"Yep."

"You get paid well for that?"

She lifted her hands as if to show me everything surrounding us was paid for by her career.

"Are there any positions available?" I asked.

"Looks like you already filled it." She smiled as she pointed to the Porsche.

Brandi and I spent the day shopping and talking. I told her about my recent exploits with my co-worker, and how much money I had made off of him.

"That's chump change," she said. "I can actually help you make that in one hour."

"Really? How?" I asked.

"I have some *friends* who have fantasies of being with me and a *real* woman at the same time. Think you may be interested?"

"Hell, yeah. You just tell me when and where."

After that night, Brandi and I spent a lot of time at The Jazz Café, where she introduced me to numerous men with more money than the Lord Almighty Himself.

Life was extremely good.

64

T'Shobi

I was sitting in the back of The Jazz Café late Tuesday night. The day before, at Justine's house, began to play vividly in my mind. I wanted to know what the hell the key was for, along with who the hell was behind it all. This ordeal had me on the verge of pure insanity.

As I sat in a secluded area of the club, watching people walk in and out, I noticed Tinisha and Brandi walking in together, looking and acting like they were the best of friends. I watched both of them for hours as they moved around the club, talking to several men.

Brandi seemed to know a lot of them, and they seemed to know her. It was strange to me, because a few months ago when I met her at the same place, it didn't appear as if she had even been there before.

"Who the hell are you?" I whispered to myself as I drank the smooth whisky from my glass.

"Hello," a tall and beautiful woman said, breaking me from my daze.

I stared at her for many seconds before speaking back. I wasn't there to pick up anyone, and I really didn't want to be bothered.

"You look famous," she said, taking it upon herself to sit down and join me at my table.

"I just have one of those faces," I responded dryly.

"My name is Tiffany."

Tiffany had already gotten on my nerves just that quick.

"Tiffany, I'm sorry, but I am definitely not in the mood for small talk, or to buy you a drink, or even to fuck you later."

I guzzled the remainder of my drink, and without waiting for a response from her, I immediately left the table and the club and went home.

Once arriving home, I continued to do what I had begun in the club—drink. I had gone back to drinking every single minute I had the opportunity. As much as I was hoping that it would keep my mind off of everything, I discovered that it had actually created more frustrations and depressions for me.

It had been weeks since I took time to visit the facility and teach music. It felt as if all the progress I made with handling my past had stopped, and now, not only had I fallen back into the past, new problems seemed to come to light.

I had actually fallen in love, or at least what I thought was love. Seeing Brandi in the faces of all those men at the club, I felt my heart twinge with hurt. I wondered if that was a one-time thing, or if she really wasn't the person I thought she was. The way she interacted with them and they way they interacted with her led me to believe they knew her secret.

As the night grew and I became drunker, my hand constantly picked up my phone with desires to call her, but I couldn't do it.

"Hello," I said into the phone, waking up to the sun shining on my face.

"T'Shobi?" a male voiced asked.

"Who is this?"

"How long have you known your girlfriend was a man?"

"Who is this?" I repeated, emerging from the floor.

"Answer my question, got-damnit!"

I grabbed my head, feeling the effects of my hangover. It seemed that each day presented a new attack. Without a word, I ended the call.

I looked at the number that called and didn't recognize it; then my phone rang again with a number I did recognize.

"Motherfucker, I asked you a question, and I demand that you give me an answer." The same irate voice was calling from Justine's house.

"Is this Frederick or Chase?" I asked.

There was a long pause.

"Chase. Now, answer my question."

"Chase, honestly, I don't think any of that is your business," I said.

"What do you mean, it's none of my business? Whatever the fuck she is, there are pictures of it and my daddy. This is my business."

"Chase, what happened between Brandi and Seth and what happened between Brandi and me are two different situations."

"Did you just call my father by his first name? That's Pastor Reynolds, a very spiritual and righteous man," he said.

"Again, Chase, my affairs are no concern of yours."

"Look here, you little faggot, I asked you a question, and I expect you to answer. If you don't answer, I promise I will tell everyone about you and your *she-male*."

"And I will explain to your wife about the time I saw you all over Tinisha in the choir room at the church. Do you think she would be happy to know that?"

He immediately hung up the phone. After that conversation with him, I knew what I was going to have to do.

The time had come, and Charlotte was no longer safe for me. It was time to move on and attempt, once again, to move forward.

"Hello, MeeMa. I'm coming home," I said immediately after she answered the phone.

65

Justine

It took a miracle for me to convince T'Shobi that he could-
n't leave until we had cleared this up. It would be damn near
impossible for any of this to go away without him around.

"Justine," he pleaded over the phone, "I can't take this shit
anymore, and with Chase calling me questioning me about
my relationship, I just can't take it."

"I will speak with Chase, but, T'Shobi, you can't run from
this. You can't keep running your entire life."

After talking with him, I immediately called Chase and
chewed him out for calling T'Shobi with his foolishness. He
was angry with me for what he called taking sides, but I had
to explain to him that his father was a screw-up, and blaming
others for what he had done would not change what he was.

After days that turned to weeks of having minimal commu-
nication with my mother, I decided that it was time to have
a talk. When I arrived home from physical therapy, she was
sitting in the living room, crocheting.

"You and Janice have all the right in the world to hate me,"
she said before I could say anything.

"Mama, we don't hate you," I said as I watched the anguish
cover her face.

"I didn't protect y'all the way a mother was supposed to."

She had a point; however, I had come to realize that all of this began in a different time. Secrets like what she and Seth's father kept were the kind that black folk were hushed on. No one spoke of the ills of a confused mind.

"Mama, it's important that we stay grounded in family now. I need you to be strong for Janice. I need you to be strong for us all."

As we sat and hugged, Janice walked in with Jonathan.

I stared at him long and hard. It amazed me how he looked more like Seth than Frederick or Chase did. The last time I saw him, he was one, and I was cursing his mother to hell.

"Hey, Aunt Justine," he said, extending his hand.

For the first time since this entire ordeal, I tried to forget the fact that my nephew was also my husband's son.

"It's good to see you again, Jonathan."

Once he sat down, I began to examine him. I watched how he interacted with my mother, with his mother, even with me. I noticed the clothes he wore. Although it was the latest in urban gear, I could tell that his taste was expensive.

"I understand that you are a gifted individual when it comes to finding people?"

"Yes, ma'am, I am," he responded.

"A friend and I need your assistance. Can you help?"

"Let me know what you need," he responded.

It was time for us to find the son-of-a-bitch that was creating all this havoc.

66

TiTi

Brandi was definitely right. She did help me make more money than I could have ever imagined. In two weeks, I had secured a rich and famous boyfriend, who provided me with anything I wanted. He never questioned my whereabouts, and I made more money running "errands" with Brandi than I had made in two years as a paralegal.

I decided to treat myself to a new car, and with Brandi, I got a great deal on a Lexus coupe. When I pulled into the parking lot of my apartment in my new car, I saw my roommate's trifling-ass boyfriend sitting in his car on the phone.

"Damn, Ti, when you going to give me a ride?"

"Tonight, when you are dreaming," I responded as I hit the remote, turning on the alarm.

"Yo, TiTi, hold up, girl," he began as he walked toward me, holding his crotch. "On the real, ma, when can I get that again?"

Obviously the fool had forgotten what happened the last time.

"Malik, I do apologize, to myself, for sinking as low as I could and making you my first."

He grabbed my arm, and I quickly removed his hand. I guess he did remember what happened last time, I thought.

"You ain't nothing but a fucking trick," he said, walking back to his car.

"I may be, but one thing's for sure: I'm a paid trick."

When I walked into my apartment, I realized that it was time to move on. I didn't need a roommate anymore, and I definitely needed to upgrade my standard of living.

After taking a shower, I was back in my car, heading to an appointment.

"What the fuck do you mean, no?" Bill asked me in the break room at work. "I've paid you damn good money for the past month, and now you cut me off?"

"Bill, dear," I began with as much sincerity as I could, "please don't get the silly idea that your money is the only money out there."

"What the hell are you talking about? Are you a prostitute?"

I smiled at his question. I never really looked at it as prostitution, but even if I had, my prostitution started with him.

"No, I am not a prostitute; however, if I must waste my time with a little-dick man, why not make it worth my while and make a couple of dollars in the process?" I said before attempting to walk away.

"Look here, you little bitch." He grabbed my arm. "You don't realize who you're fucking with!"

I stared directly into his eyes then moved my eyes toward his hand on my arm. "I would suggest that you remove your hand from my arm. The last man that grabbed me that way, his nuts were introduced to my knee."

He stared at me as if he could kill me, and I returned the stare, only stronger. He finally released me, but continued to stare.

"Bill," I said calmly, "you are the one who does not realize who they are fucking with. If you ever threaten me again, you will find out."

Before leaving work, I walked to the secretary of one of the partners of the law firm and handed her my resignation letter, stating it was effective immediately.

When I walked out of the office carrying a box containing my personal items, I saw Bill standing at the door of his office, watching me. I wanted to tell him to kiss my ass, but knowing him, he probably would have.

On my way home, I called Brandi to inform her about what had transpired that day. She had already schooled me on how to incorporate my own personal consulting firm, and had even given me the number to her accountant to set everything up. I was more than ready to take my new career and my new life to higher heights.

67

T'Shobi

"What I'm doing now is configuring your phone into my computer," Jonathan stated. "Any call you receive, I will be able to trace the location it's coming from, as well as the person that owns the device."

Although I was somewhat versed in what he was doing, it amazed me how much technology had changed the world. There was hardly anything that could be done now that could not be traced.

"Now, if it's a prepaid phone, unless they used a credit card to purchase it, basically all I would be able to do is trace where it was purchased."

I was more than anxious to get all of this out of the way so that I could leave. Justine was good for at least keeping me around until this mess was over, but I had already begun packing boxes and throwing away things I would no longer need when I left.

I knew that after all of this, my days in Charlotte were over. I didn't know where I would eventually call my new home, but I knew the places where I wouldn't.

After my conversation with Justine, I called MeeMa back to let her know that my visit home would be slightly delayed. She was disappointed, but she didn't stress it.

***

Days had gone by after Jonathan placed his mojo on my phone, and I still hadn't heard from the voice. I was beginning to believe that the voice knew what had taken place, and purposely tried not to call. Then one day, as I was sitting at the studio packing up equipment, my phone rang.

"T'Shobi, it's time," the voice said. "I need for you to go to Justine's and get the key. I will call back in an hour."

When I arrived at the house, Jonathan was sitting in the living room, typing away on his laptop.

"T'Shobi, the person behind this is currently in Charlotte. The number they are calling you from designates from Georgia. They used cash when they bought the phone, so I couldn't get any more information." He paused and took a sip of the bottled water that sat on the coffee table. "Do you know anyone in Atlanta?"

"That's where I lived before moving here."

"Well, now you have some sort of idea. Sorry I couldn't give you more."

While I was being escorted to Justine's room by her mother, my mind began to race, trying to think of any and all people that could be responsible. Only one person came to mind.

As I sat in the room alone with Justine, I mentioned to her the information that Jonathan just relayed to me.

"You have any ideas who could be behind this?" she asked.

"Yes and no."

"Care to share?" she questioned.

I shook my head.

Janice finally walked in without any greeting. She handed me the key. I looked into her eyes, and they appeared tired and worn out. I knew the feeling. I understood what it was like to have years and years of pain hit you all at once, especially when you were never able to properly heal from the initial blows.

"What's next?" Justine asked.

"I was told what I'm always told: I will receive a call when it's time for my next assignment."

We all sat in the room in complete silence, no one looking at the other. Janice walked over to the window and let out a long sigh.

"I still have nightmares of him," she said softly.

"I have them too," I replied to her, letting her know I understood her pain.

She looked toward me and our eyes met. We were like two kindred souls meeting after years of being separated.

Then the phone rang.

"T'Shobi, tomorrow you, Janice, and Justine will go to the house. Most of your questions will be answered then."

As soon as the called ended, Jonathan ran in, carrying his laptop.

"I have a location," he said excitedly.

68

Seth

"Seth, my dear friend," my captor began, "have you groomed yourself properly? I would hate for your family to find you looking as bad as you do right now. They, along with T'Shobi, will be there tomorrow to *save* you. By the way, there's a special object in the travel bag that you may want to consider using, just in case," he said, laughing before hanging up.

When the call ended, my heart began to beat tremendously fast. I had noticed the object when I opened it. I had thought about using it earlier.

The night before was a long and treacherous one. The drugs that were in my food and water didn't help me sleep. I stared long and hard at the gun that had been placed in the bag, and several times during the night, I thought about using it. I didn't want to be found anymore. I was ready to go and meet my maker for Him to give me my sentence for eternity.

All of my sins had finally come to light. My family was aware of what I was. My sons, I was more than certain, knew what their father was. I would no longer be able to serve in a church again. I had no other skills, and I would surely go to jail for years for embezzlement.

I held the gun in my hand. There was no longer any reason to live.

69

T'Shobi

After Jonathan gave me the information, I literally ran out of the house and jumped in my car. I was headed back to the house that I was instructed to not go to until the next day. I was about to find out who was behind all of this and settle this once and for all.

As I got closer, something told me to wait until dark. I was running off adrenaline and I wasn't thinking straight. I needed to be calm and relaxed when I made contact. Although I had an idea of who it was, I still wasn't a hundred percent sure.

I made my usual two stops then went home.

The time moved slowly. I was ready for night to fall so that I could begin my mission. I called Justine back to let her know what my plans were.

"Maybe you shouldn't go alone," she advised.

"I will be fine," I said before hanging up.

For the next several hours, I drank and smoked in moderation. I wanted to make sure that I could still think quickly if something did jump off.

I circled the street a few times to check for any signs of

trouble. I decided to park my car two streets over and walk back to the house. Before getting out of my car, I popped my trunk to retrieve my gun. I didn't like guns, but at the same time, I wasn't going to go in half-assed either.

I first looked into the house I had visited several times to retrieve packages, but the house that was my main concern was directly across the street. That's where Jonathan had found the signal from the phone. As I began to walk across the street, I noticed three cars: a Cadillac with Georgia license tags, a Lexus with new dealer tags, and a car I knew well, Brandi's Jaguar.

Although stunned, I couldn't really say that I was in total shock.

I searched around the house, trying to get a good look and hoping that I wasn't seen. I could hear soft music and a few moans, and even some loud screams. I knew two of the screams well. I felt my body fill with rage. It wasn't a rage of jealousy, but one of hate and disgust for feeling betrayed by two selfish bastards.

After searching outside of the house for several moments, I found an unlocked window to climb through. As soon as I entered the house, I heard a third voice. This one wasn't familiar.

I slowly and quietly made my way upstairs, and to my surprise, the door to the room the three of them were in was open, exposing their act for me to see. I felt disgusted and shocked, especially after recognizing the person behind that third voice.

They didn't hear me. Not one of them realized that they had an audience, until I pulled out my gun. When they heard me cock it, they all stopped. All were stunned at who stood before them.

70

TiTi

When I walked out of my room, Trice and Malik were sitting on the couch watching TV, and in my opinion, both of them looked pathetic.

For half a second, I felt nauseated that I had even lowered myself to sleep with Malik.

"Trice, just to give you a heads up, I will be moving soon," I said, walking toward the door to leave. "By the way, girl, I don't see how in the world you could want to stay with a dead fuck like that thing beside you."

"I knew it!" I heard Trice yelling as I was walking down the stairs.

When I walked into Brandi's place, she was on the phone. I could tell by the serious look on her face and the tone of her voice that she was taking care of business. I plunged down on the couch in the bonus room and turned on the TV.

After about five minutes, she walked into the room, still on the phone.

"Wanna make some money tonight?" she whispered as she covered the phone with her hand.

"Is a pig's ass pork?" I asked, laughing.

"Okay, I will see you in an hour. Mind if I bring a friend?" she said to whomever she was talking to. "Okay, cool, see you then."

We arrived at the house to meet her client in separate cars. I looked at it and the surrounding houses. There was nothing spectacular about them. They were plain and simple.

"Are you sure this person has enough money for the both of us?"

She giggled at my comment.

"Looks like I created a little monster." She laughed some more. "Yes, he can take care of both of us very well. He's here in town to take care of some business. This is a house he uses while here in town."

The house was very modest, and it looked just as she said, like someone was just here to handle business and leave. When we walked in, I was almost shocked to see who was sitting on the couch, wearing nothing but a T-shirt and boxer shorts.

"Randall, this is my friend, TiTi. TiTi, this is Randall Cole."

"Bishop Randall Cole?" I asked, surprised.

For years, Tinisha had seen this man on TV, preaching his heart out. He was actually one of her favorites.

"In the flesh, baby girl," he said, standing up from the couch. He walked over to the mini bar and poured a drink. "Can I offer you anything?" he said, smiling at me.

"Yes, whatever that is you're having," I said, still in shock of who I was talking to.

"So, TiTi, are you the real thing, or do you dangle too?" he said, looking toward my southern region.

"You are a mess, Randall," Brandi interrupted, laughing. "She's the real thing. I thought maybe you would enjoy the both of us tonight."

"Girl, that's why I love you so much. You know how to make an old man's everything jump up and dance a jig."

After several moments of idle chit-chat and drinking, we walked upstairs to a surprisingly spacious master bedroom.

In the few short weeks of running these types of errands with Brandi, I assumed that the routine would be the same; but this time, it was a little different.

Randall got completely naked, and then got on all fours.

"Come here, girl, and get in front of me," he directed. "Yeah, yeah, that's right. Let daddy taste that good stuff."

As he began to do his do with me, I looked behind him to see Brandi doing him—and she was doing him well. Each push she gave, he sucked my clit even harder, making me cum instantly, several times.

"Oh, yeah, baby," he moaned while still sucking my clit. "Keep making that water fall."

We were at it for nearly two hours before taking a short break. As we lay in the bed, Brandi on one side of him and me on the other, he went on and on, telling us that was one of the best nights he'd had with two people in a long time.

"Your time with us was just one of the best, and not the best?" Brandi questioned. "Randall, you offend us."

"Oh, sweetie, no need to be offended. As a matter of fact, I'm giving you double what you asked for—as long as we do it a few more times before you leave."

I wanted to ask what was double, but Brandi gave me my answer before I could ask.

"You down to make fifty-thousand each, Ti?"

Of course she knew my answer.

***

Again we were back to our fun, but this time instead of his tongue, it was his penis inside of me, while Brandi remained in her position behind him, screwing the ever-loving life out of the bishop.

With each thrust she made in him, he made an equally powerful thrust in me. A few times, somewhere deep within, I could hear Tinisha crying in disbelief that this well known and very famous preacher, who was viewed daily on TV by millions, was a straight-up freak. I, on the other hand, was enjoying every bit of it. Knowing that just this night alone could almost pay off my car, I wouldn't have given a damn if it was the Pope himself with his dick inside of me.

The party continued throughout the night. Around midnight, he wanted to go one more round with us. About fifteen minutes into it, we were interrupted by the scariest sound I had ever heard.

Click, Click.

When I looked back to see T'Shobi standing over the bed, aiming the gun at all three of us, I came close to dying of a heart attack.

71

Seth

The gun was definitely my choice. I refused to face the world in shame. I refused to live the rest of my life locked up. The past eight months alone had damn near killed me; I didn't want to think about what being in a prison with murderers and thieves would be like.

I retrieved the gun from the bag and checked the barrel. I took four bullets out, leaving one. I then placed the gun on the table and began to pray. I wasn't sure if God could or would be willing to hear my prayer.

My life was based on a lie. Every aspect of it, from the time I was fifteen, was lie. I thought about my father and wondered how he would view his baby boy now. Would he still protect me the best way he knew how, or would he give me the proper guidance that he should have almost forty years earlier? At that moment, it no longer mattered. I realized that the things I had become were not the things that God would forgive me for. But how could He? I never asked Him for forgiveness.

I closed the barrel of the gun then aimed it toward my head.

"I'm sorry, Frederick," I whispered then pulled the trigger.

Click.

"I'm sorry, Chase."

Click.

"I'm sorry, Jonathan."
Click.
"I'm sorry, Janice."

72

T'Shobi

"T'Shobi? What the hell are you doing here? How did you find me?"

I didn't say a word. I just watched Bishop Randall Cole, Tinisha, and Brandi watch me with total fear in their eyes.

"T'Shobi, it's not what you think," Brandi said, watching the gun I was pointing at them.

"Shut the fuck up!" I responded.

"T'Shobi, son, please?" Randall pleaded.

"What did you call me?" I asked, feeling the rage of twenty-seven years rush through body, ready to raise so much hell that the devil himself would have to sit back and say damn. "I know this fool didn't just call me son."

The three of them remained on the bed, unsure of what to do. They were all scared, and I loved the power I was feeling at the moment.

From the look on Tinisha's face, I could tell she was completely dumb to what was going on.

"Your crazy ass don't even know what you got yourself into," I said to her as the tears rolled down her face.

"T'Shobi, let the ladies go and we can talk about this man to man."

"Randall, there's only one lady in here," I said.

"Just let them go so that we can talk."

I stared at the two of them. I wanted to shoot Brandi right there, and actually, at the moment, I was ready to. But who I really wanted was the bastard that orchestrated the entire mess.

"Go," I told them.

After they scrambled for their clothes, I heard them run down the stairs and eventually walk out the door.

"So, where is Seth? In the house across the street?" I asked.

He nodded his head.

"So, what was all of this for? Did he do something to you? Did I do something to you? Why?" I wanted to know.

"You weren't supposed to leave me, T'Shobi. You were mine! All mine!"

"What are you, some kind of new fool?" I asked, disgusted. "You are telling me that you set out to ruin families because I left you and your freak-ass wife?"

"You were mine. Can't you see that? I love you."

Suddenly, that rage that was building up had reached its high and was at the point of explosion. I felt my hand tighten up on the gun, and before I knew anything, my finger pulled the trigger.

Pow!

I stared at him as the urine began to flow quickly from his penis and onto the bed he was still sitting on.

"You are one sick son of a bitch." I began watching him shiver. "You get the fuck out of here and make sure I never hear from you again, or next time, the bullet won't miss you on purpose."

"T'Shobi, wait," he pleaded yet again.

I aimed the gun back at him. "What part of not hearing from you again did you not understand?"

When I got outside, the cool night air did nothing to calm the heat that had built up inside of me. I was confused and flustered about everything. My life was nothing but one chaotic roller coaster. Nothing seemed to work in my favor. It was too much for one person to handle without breaking down and just going crazy.

I looked back at the house where Randall was. I still couldn't believe the measures he took to create all of this because he felt that I belonged to him. I wanted to kill him for using the word *love* to me alone. I was finally convinced that there was no such thing as love anymore.

When I made it across the street to the other house, I retrieved the key out of my pocket and used it to open the door. The house was empty. I walked around, but there appeared to be no life.

"Seth," I called out, but received no answer.

I searched the entire house, and still nothing. I walked into the kitchen and noticed a door at the far end. I heard the sounds of a TV coming. When I opened the door, I saw Seth's body lying in pool of blood.

"Justine," I began over the phone, "he's dead!"

73

Justine

I don't know why, but hearing T'Shobi tell me that Seth was lying in a pool of blood kind of pissed me off. I wanted to be the one to shoot his ass.

"Did you shoot him?" I asked him.

"He was already dead when I got here."

"So, did you find out who was behind all of this?"

"Yes," he said softly. "Randall Cole."

"Bishop Randall Cole?" I asked, stunned.

"Yes."

After T'Shobi explained to me the entire ordeal, I began to get sick to my stomach, realizing that I was in a similar situation with him. I was disgusted with myself, and couldn't believe that I allowed Seth to frustrate me so badly over the years that I had failed to use my good common sense and not make the stupid mistakes I had made.

"Are you still leaving?" I asked him.

"Yes."

"When are you leaving?"

"Soon," he responded sharply.

"Will I see you before you leave?"

"I doubt it," he said before hanging up the phone.

After conversing with him, I called for Janice to come into the room so that I could inform her of Seth's death.

We both cried in one another's arms. The tears were not tears of sadness, but tears of joy and triumph. My sister's evil was now gone. We could finally start on mending our family. She could finally have some relief. She could finally feel peace. Or could she?

74

TiTi

When I made it back to my apartment, I was still scared as hell. I had to admit that whether I was Tinisha or TiTi, that moment, with T'Shobi pointing the gun at me, was the most frightening experience I ever had. The look he had in his eyes was the look of a killer.

It was almost two in the morning when I walked into my room to notice that it had been totally destroyed. I couldn't believe what I was looking at. My clothes were torn and spread across the room. Nail polish covered the carpet and the clothes that she didn't rip apart.

I walked to the kitchen closet and found the bat Trice tried to scare me with weeks earlier. I walked to her room, opened the door, and began beating both of those fools until I saw blood coming from them.

"Wrong bitch, wrong night," I said as I walked out of the room as they moaned.

I called Brandi to see if I could stay with her for the night.

The next morning, the two of us were sitting on her couch, drinking coffee and watching the news. We were both still shaken up from the events from the night before.

She went on to tell me her small role in the "set-up" as she called it.

"Randall hired me to seduce T'Shobi, to soften him up, and to set up Seth."

"Pastor Reynolds?" I asked, confused. "What does he have to do with any of this?"

"He and T'Shobi were lovers."

That stunned me. I remembered months ago when Tinisha caught Justine leaving his apartment.

"T'Shobi was having an affair with Justine too," I said softly.

"I know. When he lived in Atlanta, he was with Randall, as well as with his wife."

I thought about T'Shobi's words to me as he pointed the gun: "Your crazy ass don't even know what you got yourself into."

She talked for over an hour about the entire ordeal, and it was overwhelming. The news was on, but we didn't really notice, until the reporter said something that caught our attention.

"Pastor Seth Reynolds," the reporter began, "well-known pastor of the mega church New Deliverance, who had been missing for eight months, was found dead in the basement of this house behind me. After reports of gunshots, police came to investigate and discovered him lying in a pool of blood. Police are calling the shooting a suicide."

I recognized the house. It was the one across the street from where we were less than six hours earlier.

75

TiTi

One Year Later

It's amazing how much can happen in a year.

My life had been altered, and there was no way I would return to the life I once thought—or better yet, the one my mother told me—was the right way to live.

No longer was I concerned about living recklessly. As a matter of fact, it was never me that felt that way, but a girl who used to be known as Tinisha. She was the one that spent hours upon hours chasing one man to love her. It was she who prayed to a God that obviously never heard her. It was Tinisha who had the overly obsessive mother that sheltered her, never allowing her the opportunity to experience a real life. That was not me. That was never me.

Although I had always been around, I was suppressed and not allowed to surface, until Tinisha made the mistake of acting out of character and trying to do something I would have done. The only difference was that I would have succeeded. I am not ashamed to state the facts. I am far from being beyond self-praise. It's a proven fact: I am one bad bitch.

Some people would probably say that I was created from the ashes of rejection, but how can something already there be created? It was predestined for me to become who I am.

My best friend, Brandi, once said something to me about all of us having that one person that changes the path that we walk. Honestly, I don't know if I believe that. We all have the right at any given moment to change what direction we want to go. It's basically just up to us to choose.

Tinisha Jackson would never quit her job making twenty-five thousand a year and receiving piss-poor insurance. But me, hell, I can make twenty-five thousand dollars in one hour, and if I get sick, I have a doctor who would be more than happy to give me a checkup, along with a check, and send me on my merry way.

Life is good. No, life is great! And for those of you who still may not know me, let me properly introduce myself:

My name is TiTi. Ms. Jackson if you nasty!

76

Justine

Life after Seth was hard at first. The reporters, the police, the church—everyone camped out in front of our house, seeking information.

The strain was difficult, not to mention losing the house, cars, and bank accounts that were seized due to Seth's years of just plain foolishness. There were days that I wished he was still living so that I could kill him.

Jonathan was surprisingly helpful in getting us all back on financial track. Two months after Seth's death, he invited us all, my mother, sons, their wives and children, and me to move to Florida to live with him and Janice.

When I saw the house he owned, I couldn't help but believe how modest she was when she told me that he was wealthy. He was filthy rich. Jonathan was also instrumental in providing me with one of the top physical therapy facilities in the country. In less than six months, I was actually walking again.

Although the situation was very difficult for everyone, Jonathan, Chase, and Frederick were still brothers, and the actions of their father were those that he created, not them.

There were times that I thought about T'Shobi. I even wanted to call him a few times, but I came to realize that we knew each other in another life, another time that no longer existed.

It was not a big secret that I had stopped praying many years earlier, but often I found myself getting on my knees and praying for T'Shobi, hoping that he found a peace that he had searched for his entire life. He deserved it.

77

T'Shobi

It took almost a miracle, but MeeMa finally decided to move into my house in Atlanta. I guess after her son Russell died, it was easier for her, and it helped to ease the pain of not being in the city that had given her so many memories of her son.

"Why didn't you ever tell me he did things to you?" she asked one day as I was sitting with her before leaving for my next city to find yet another new beginning.

"I thought I loved him. I was a confused child," I told her solemnly.

I'm a confused man, too, were the thoughts flowing through my mind.

I tried not to think too much on my life anymore. When I truly thought about it, there were many positive points as well, and it was time for me to begin to concentrate on those.

After finding Seth dead, I was on my way to Montgomery the next morning. The five-hour drive seemed to go faster than I had expected. Once I arrived in town, I was amazed at how much had changed in ten years. When I left at seventeen, I vowed that I would never come back again.

I decided to stop and get something to eat before going to MeeMa's house, but my sense of direction led me somewhere else.

"I can't do this," I whispered as I stared at the broken-down house.

I was looking at my past. It wasn't the beautiful home that once seemed happy. It looked like a house torn and beaten, just like my heart.

I gently knocked on the door, hoping that no one would answer.

"Yes? May I help you?" a young lady wearing a nursing uniform asked me.

"I'm looking for Mrs. Pratt," I said softly. "Does she still live here?"

The young nurse stared at me for moments as if she was trying to figure out if she knew me.

"You're T'Shobi Wells, aren't you?" she said with excitement.

I nodded my head.

"Mr. Wells, I have all of your CDs. I can't believe it's really you. God has really anointed you with a powerful gift of music. I heard that you were from here, but I didn't believe it."

As we stood at the threshold of the door, I could hear someone yelling from the back.

"Girl, what is all of that commotion?"

I recognized the voice immediately.

The young lady escorted me to the back room. As we walked through the house, I noticed there were not many changes to the house since I had been there years earlier.

As we passed a piano with several pictures on it, one stood out.

"Are you okay?" the nurse asked me when she noticed I stopped.

I pointed at the picture. "That's me," I said softly.

"Are you serious?" she said with more excitement. "I've always wondered who that little boy was. I asked Ms. Pratt once, but she began to cry. I assumed it was a son that had died or something."

"He did die," I whispered.

She slowly opened the door, and lying on the medical bed in the middle of the room, I saw her.

"T'Shobi," she said, knowing who I was without me having to tell her. "I'm sorry."

I stared at her for moments before moving toward her. In those few seconds, my entire childhood flashed before my face. I felt all of the pain and frustration rush through my body, and suddenly, I felt a peace.

"Can you ever forgive me?" she asked, crying.

I wanted to say no and tell her how my life had been since the very first day she stole my life away from me. I wanted to tell her everything, but looking at her broken, knowing that she had paid her debt for her actions against me, I knew it was time for me to forgive and begin to heal.

I moved closer to her. Tears ran down my face as I hugged the first person who helped to create the man I had become.

"Now we both can heal," I whispered.

78

Brandi

It took me an entire year to gain the nerve to go back home. I was unsure what to expect, but it was something I knew I needed to do to heal, or discover that my healing would never come. My life had been a difficult one, and I knew that many of my actions as an adult were based on what happened to me as a child.

Sitting in my car looking at the house I used to call home, I wondered what was going on inside at that moment.

The house wasn't anything special, just plain and unassuming, but I knew better. I knew everything that went on in there.

I sat for hours, watching men and women go in and out. Some came out staggering from the drugs they bought; some came out happy from the great sex they thought they were getting. Some were just happy to feel that they were a part of anything, regardless of how fucked up it may have been.

As I continued to watch the house, I saw a young boy around the age of six or seven come out of the front door. I watched him play in front of the house. He looked innocent. He reminded me of someone from many years ago: me.

A few moments passed before I saw an older woman come out of the house to get the boy. I knew her. She looked the same, but older and a few pounds heavier.

"Brandon, bring your ass inside," she yelled.

As I watched him, I suddenly had a flashback. He reminded me of the person I was almost thirty years ago.

As he ran up to her, she popped him on his butt then pulled him inside the house. The two of them came out moments later and got into an old, beat-down Jeep Cherokee. I decided to follow them.

Thirty minutes later, I saw her pushing the little boy in the shopping cart through the Wal-Mart. After observing the two of them for several moments, I decided to make my move.

"Oh, excuse me," I said after "accidentally" bumping into her cart.

"Oh, no, excuse me, ma'am."

"What a cute little boy," I said, looking at the boy playing with a toy car. "What's his name?"

"Thanks. His name is Brandon," she responded.

"What made you choose to name him that?" I questioned.

She became silent and her eyes saddened. "Excuse me, ma'am, but I have to finish my shopping and get back home."

"You didn't answer my question," I said as I grabbed her arm.

"Do I know you?"

I gave her a curt smile as I stared long into her eyes. "You tell me. Do you know me?" I asked.

She began to stare at me hard, and her eyes revealed to me that she did. Tears began to stream down her face.

"I suggest that you don't be home tonight," I said.

"Who be that lady, Ma?" I heard my little brother ask my mother as I walked away, prepared to handle my business.

Later that night, as I sat in my car, I noticed my mother

sneaking out of the house with Brandon. As she was getting into the car, she began looking around as if she was looking for someone. I knew that she was looking to see if I was nearby.

After she left, I grabbed the steel pipe out of the trunk, and then made my way to the house, the hell that I once called home.

Walking across the dead grass, my life as a child and teenager began to play as if it were a Lifetime movie.

My father was a pimp; my mother, one of his ladies. I never knew my father's real name. His ladies called him Sugar Bear. Everyone else just knew him as Sugar, but there wasn't a damn thing sweet about that nigger. He was nothing but a snake. He didn't only pimp out his ladies, he also had a few men, and he had me.

When I was fifteen, I was sitting at the dinner table, doing homework, when he summoned me to his room.

"You know what, boy? You would make a cute-ass girl," he said, throwing a wig and dress at me. "I have this client, an old white man I need you to go see tonight. Make sure you wear that wig and dress. You hear?" My orders were given, and my life was set.

When I opened the front door, I heard the faint sound of a TV, and I heard him talking on the phone.

"Bitch, don't fuck with me or my money. Do you hear me?" he yelled. "I will kill you if you don't get that shit right this time."

I walked slowly into the room with the pipe ready to do damage. After he hung up the phone, I watched him as he went back to where the TV was playing.

"Lilly, where you at?" he called out for my mother. "Lilly, got-damnit, woman, where you at?"

"Lilly's gone," I said, staring at him.

"Who the fuck is you? Damn, baby, you fine. Wanna make some money?"

I looked at him with disgust. "Trust, Sugar, the money you make in a year does not compare to what I make in a day," I said.

He stared long and hard at me.

"Brandon?"

"Brandi now, thanks to you," I said.

"Wha-wha . . . How you been?"

I stared at the shell of a man that used to scare me. "How the fuck do you think I've been?"

He quickly tried to get up. I knew that he was running for his gun, so I ran to him, raising the pipe, and I began swinging. He tried to get away, but the pipe connected directly to his temple and he dropped.

I looked at him for moments before I decided to drag his body to the ditch that was fifteen feet behind the house in the woods. I didn't want my baby brother to come home to see his daddy dead in the house. I wanted him to have a real chance to live a life of normalcy, something I never had the opportunity to do. My mother chose to name him after me with the hopes of doing it right this time, and I chose to kill that son-of-a-bitch to help make that happen.

I stared at his body lying in the ditch, looking as if he were in peace. It happened too quickly; he didn't suffer at all. I'd wanted him to suffer in the same manner in which I had for so long.

"Damn you!" I said aloud as I looked over his dead body. His eyes remained open, almost laughing at me. "Damn you!"

I walked through the dark woods, feeling more rage than when I began my journey earlier that morning. For some reason, I thought that the sun would suddenly jump out into the sky and give me the shine that I had been deprived of for so long.

As I arrived at my car, I stopped, turned slowly, and raised my eyes to look in the direction I had just traveled. I fell to the ground, my knees aching in pain as I slumped in prayer, hoping that somehow, God would allow me to repent one more time for my already long list of indiscretions.

The next morning, I sat in the hotel room preparing to head back to Charlotte, and I began to think about Sugar. I wondered if he had not made me into who I had become, would I have still been able to make the money that I was making? I wondered if I would have become a clone of him and become a pimp myself. Wait, I did become a pimp. I had ladies, and "ladies" working for me now.

It's funny when you think about it. The first person that does something positive, or maybe even fucked up, in your life, is actually the one that helps to create the person you become.

"Dirty Little Secret, Incorporated," I sang into the phone after viewing the name of my girlfriend and business partner, TiTi, on the caller ID.

"Girl, you won't believe where I am," she said with excitement.

"I betchu I can," I said with total assurance.

Book Club Discussion Questions

1. How much of T'Shobi's past do you think played a role in the man he became?

2. What role did Tinisha's mother play in her development?

3. What were your overall thoughts of Justine?

4. When did you discover that Brandi was Brandon?

5. Describe in detail your overall thoughts of Seth.

6. Brandi stated the actions of others cause us to become who we are. Do you believe that?

7. Do you believe that Tinisha will ever return, or has TiTi taken complete control?

8. What were your overall thoughts of *The First Person?*

ORDER FORM
URBAN BOOKS, LLC
78 E. Industry Ct
Deer Park, NY 11729

Name: (please print):_____

Address: _____

City/State: _____

Zip: _____

QTY	TITLES	PRICE
	16 ½ On The Block	$14.95
	16 On The Block	$14.95
	Betrayal	$14.95
	Both Sides Of The Fence	$14.95
	Cheesecake And Teardrops	$14.95
	Denim Diaries	$14.95
	Happily Ever Now	$14.95
	Hell Has No Fury	$14.95
	If It Isn't love	$14.95
	Last Breath	$14.95
	Loving Dasia	$14.95
	Say It Ain't So	$14.95

Shipping and Handling - add $3.50 for 1st book then $1.75 for each additional book.

Please send a check payable to:

Urban Books, LLC

Please allow 4 - 6 weeks for delivery

ORDER FORM
URBAN BOOKS, LLC
78 E. Industry Ct
Deer Park, NY 11729

Name: (please print):_____

Address: _____

City/State: _____

Zip: _____

QTY	TITLES	PRICE
	The Cartel	$14.95
	The Cartel#2	$14.95
	The Dopeman's Wife	$14.95
	The Prada Plan	$14.95
	Gunz And Roses	$14.95
	Snow White	$14.95
	A Pimp's Life	$14.95
	Hush	$14.95
	Little Black Girl Lost 1	$14.95
	Little Black Girl Lost 2	$14.95
	Little Black Girl Lost 3	$14.95
	Little Black Girl Lost 4	$14.95

Shipping and Handling - add $3.50 for 1st book then $1.75 for each additional book.
Please send a check payable to:
Urban Books, LLC
Please allow 4 - 6 weeks for delivery

ORDER FORM
URBAN BOOKS, LLC
78 E. Industry Ct
Deer Park, NY 11729

Name: (please print): _____

Address: _____

City/State: _____

Zip: _____

QTY	TITLES	PRICE
	A Man's Worth	$14.95
	Abundant Rain	$14.95
	Battle Of Jericho	$14.95
	By The Grace Of God	$14.95
	Dance Into Destiny	$14.95
	Divorcing The Devil	$14.95
	Forsaken	$14.95
	Grace And Mercy	$14.95
	Guilty & Not Guilty Of Love	$14.95
	His Woman, His Wife His Widow	$14.95
	Illusion	$14.95
	The LoveChild	$14.95

Shipping and Handling - add $3.50 for 1st book then $1.75 for each additional book.

Please send a check payable to:

Urban Books, LLC

Please allow 4 - 6 weeks for delivery

ORDER FORM
URBAN BOOKS, LLC
78 E. Industry Ct
Deer Park, NY 11729

Name: (please print):_____

Address: _____

City/State: _____

Zip: _____

QTY	TITLES	PRICE

Shipping and Handling - add $3.50 for 1st book then $1.75 for each additional book.
Please send a check payable to:
   Urban Books, LLC
Please allow 4 - 6 weeks for delivery

Notes